Also by Zilpha Keatley Snyder

UNTIL THE
CELEBRATION

UNTIL THE CELEBRATION

Zilpha Keatley Snyder

ILLUSTRATED BY
Alton Raible

Atheneum 1977 *New York*

Library of Congress Cataloging in Publication Data

Snyder, Zilpha Keatley.
    Until the celebration.

    Third book of a trilogy; 1st book: Below the
root, 2d book: And all between.
    Summary: At a time when the Erdlings are to
reenter Green-sky, mounting tension is eventually
soothed by two children who have become symbols of
the unification.
    [1. Fantasy] I. Raible, Alton,
II. Title.
PZ7.S68522Un [Fic] 76-40984
ISBN 0-689-30572-9

To Larry

The Peoples

The KINDAR	the people of Green-sky, gentle and passive and directed in all things by—
The OL-ZHAAN	revered and worshipped as holy beings, gifted with great wisdom and Spirit-force, but in reality only human and ignorant of the existence of—
The GEETS-KEL	a secret and select inner society of Ol-zhaan, who for generations had kept the secret of the true nature of—
The PASH-SHAN	monstrous creatures who lived imprisoned below the barrier Root, but who were, in reality, only—
The ERDLINGS	descendants of banished Kindar.

The People

The CHILDREN	*Teera Eld*—the Erdling child escaped to Green-sky and *Pomma D'ok*—the Kindar child, younger sister of Raamo.
The REJOYNERS	*Raamo D'ok*—the Spirit-gifted young novice Ol-zhaan.

Genaa D'anhk—Raamo's brilliant and beautiful fellow novice.

Neric D'akt—rebellious young Ol-zhaan whose suspicions led to the search for the truth about the Pash-Shan.

D'ol Falla—the ancient and honored Ol-zhaan whose searching Spirit led her to join the young rebels.

Hiro D'anhk—Genaa's father, honored Kindar scholar and leader, newly rescued from banishment.

Kanna Eld and Herd Eld—Teera's parents, sent to Orbora as Erdling ambassadors.

And OTHERS

D'ol Regle—novice-master of the Ol-zhaan, who abducted the children in order to force the Rejoyners to give up their plans for bringing Kindar and Erdlings together.

D'ol Salaat—novice Ol-zhaan and ardent follower of D'ol Regle.

D'ol Wassou—Ol-zhaan and Geets-kel, but among the first to embrace the cause of the Rejoyners.

D'ol Birta—another Geets-kel who became dedicated to the Rejoyning.

Hearba D'ok—the parents of
  and   Raamo and Pomma.
Valdo D'ok

Axon Befal—leader of the Nekom, an Erdling society dedicated to vengeance.

UNTIL THE
CELEBRATION

Uniforce was dead. It was a sad truth that had been accepted for generations, along with the certainty that all of the gifts of the Spirit were waning. Even such birthright gifts as pensing had long been limited to the very young. Infants born, as Kindar had always been, with the ability to communicate freely beyond the use of voice, seldom reached their sixth year with even a trace of Spirit-skill. And uniforce, always rare and unpredictable, had become no more than a legend.

But then, as the powerful D'ol Regle had turned towards an ancient tool-of-violence to threaten his opponents, two captive children had stretched out their hands and a great force was released. Before the eyes of the secret society the Geets-kel, the ugly metal instrument—blunt-snouted, heavy—in its gleaming mass and in the dread weight of its purpose, rose from the table as lightly as a mistborne blossom on a morning breeze. As the weapon sank gently down to rest at the children's feet, someone breathed the word "uniforce," and another repeated it, and then the Geets-kel were on their feet, their arms outstretched in the Kindar gesture of reverence.

CHAPTER ONE

S ince early childhood, the farheights had been Raamo's refuge in times of mind-pain, and in the evening of the day that came to be called the Rejoyning, he climbed far and fast. Far above temples and nid-places, rampways and ladders, he pushed his way upward with almost frantic haste, through clustered endbranches and sun-stunted webbings of tendril. At last he stopped in the swaying fragile endgrowth and fashioned a resting place of leaf and twig. Lying there with only a lacy fan of rooftree frond between him and the endless sky, he stilled his racing mind and sent his Spirit in search of Peace and understanding.

The day was already fading, and the clouds of first rain were beginning to gather. Soon the soft gray blanket would be complete, and the planet would be shut away from the cold eternity of space, enclosed and comforted by soothing rain-song, warm and light and generous in gifts of growth and greening. It was a time and place of Joy and peacefulness, and, as always, Raamo joyed in the high, clear silence and the fragile hopeful reach of the high forest. But this time the Joy was not deep

5

enough to drown the fear that he had fled.

The fear had begun only a short time before, there on the stage of the Geets-kel's secret meeting chamber, at a moment when all the others were still caught up in a great wave of hope and faith. The scene returned to Raamo with such vividness that it blotted out the sky; and when he closed his eyes against it, it continued, a clear and detailed imaging against the dark curtain of his eyelids.

He saw the children, as he had seen them there, bound and helpless, against the far wall of the high stage—his sister Pomma, great-eyed and fragile, and the sturdy, vivid Erdling child, Teera Eld. He saw their outstretched hands and felt again the great rushing force that had lifted the ancient weapon from where it lay and sent it drifting through the air. And he felt once more the wonder and awe, and the wildly contagious surge of courage and hope, as the Geets-kel had one by one stepped forward to pledge themselves to the cause of truth.

It had been one of the Geets-kel, the old man D'ol Wassou, who had spoken first. "I have seen a miracle," he said, "and to me, its meaning is clear. I wish to pledge myself to the reuniting of the people of Green-sky, Kindar with Erdling, and to the wisdom of D'ol Falla and the vision of D'ol Raamo. And to the great gift that has been restored to us by these children—one Erdling and one Kindar—both Spirit-blessed and holy, as once we all were, in the early days before a part of us was shut away to live in prison, below the Root."

Then others among the Geets-kel came forward to speak, naming Pomma and Teera beautiful and blessed and holy. And many spoke also of Raamo, praising him and calling him prophet and seer.

It had been D'ol Birta who spoke of the "Answer Song," calling it a true prophecy, and of Raamo himself, as a foreseer, akin to the ancient prophets who had guided the people in the early days.

Remembering how he had sung the song, a nonsense chant of children, in hopeless desperation because no other answer had come to him when D'ol Falla had begged him for a foretelling, he flinched with anguish. He could see now how it might seem a foretelling. The words could have many meanings:

> And all between becomes among,
> And we are they and old is young,
> And earth is sky,
> And all is one.

And yet, he knew that he had not sung it as a revelation, but only as children had sung it for generations—haunted by its surprising rhythms and by the mysterious uncertainties of its meaning.

The memory was acutely disturbing, as was also the memory of the children, still standing against the tendril-woven wall, with the tool-of-violence at their feet—their small faces tensed by a strange bright excitement, as they listened to the words of praise and adoration.

But then Kanna, the mother of Teera, had gone to them, and Raamo had run to Pomma. Loosened from their bonds and held and caressed, they had clung like infants, whimpering with relief and Joy.

It was then that Hiro D'anhk had stepped forward and suggested a ceremony of welcome be made for the Erdlings—for Teera and for Kanna and Herd, also. The Geets-kel agreed eagerly, and so the ceremony was

7

made, and then the planning had begun—plans for the Rejoyning, a name given by D'ol Falla to this time of truth and reunion—and great change. It had been decided that the changes would begin at once, on the morning of the next day, when the truth would be taken to the leaders of the Kindar.

It had been D'ol Falla who insisted that the Kindar be told first. It had seemed to the others, and in the beginning, even to Raamo, himself, that the first meeting should be with the Ol-zhaan. Such an ordering seemed not only proper, but prudent—for although the Ol-zhaan were not, as the Kindar believed, all-wise and all-powerful, they were trained for leadership and far better equipped by knowledge and background to deal with the problems that were sure to lay ahead. But D'ol Falla had insisted that the first meeting should be with guild and grund-masters, scholars and instructors, with those who were most honored and respected within the Kindar society. And D'ol Falla had prevailed.

Remembering how she had prevailed, Raamo smiled, forgetting his anxiety for the moment, in his Love and admiration for the tiny ancient woman. Truly, she had not reached her high position among the Ol-zhaan by accident. Using the force of the Geets-kel's newfound faith and blending it skillfully with the old established authority of her high position, she had led them to a reluctant agreement. That very evening the summons would be sent to the Kindar leaders, and in the morning the truth-telling would take place, in the great meeting hall of Orbora.

It had been then, when those final plans were made, that Raamo had first noticed the faces of some of the men and women of the Geets-kel stiffen with fear. They had turned in those moments from the ecstasy of their faith in the miracle they had witnessed, to the grim possibilities of its consequences. From their faith in the power that had flowed from the children—to the fact that they, themselves, must stand revealed as deceivers and betrayers. It was not until then, reminded by thoughts of guilt and blame, that they had remembered D'ol Regle, and seen that he was gone.

Raamo had not seen him go, nor had anyone else. Sometime before, probably during the ceremony of welcome, the novice-master must have slipped behind the tapestries at the rear of the stage, through the small robing room that lay behind it, and out into the open forest. But after a brief moment of shocked indignation, most of the Geets-kel seemed to believe that D'ol Regle's disappearance was of little consequence.

"What does it matter?" someone had asked.

"Yes, what harm can he do now? He has probably run back to his palace to nurse his wounded pride. And if he has run away into the forest, what harm can he do there—alone and in disgrace?"

But Raamo was afraid. His fear had grown at D'ol Regle's disappearance, but it had begun earlier. It had started as a dim and distant warning, a sense of turnings being made down dangerous pathways, and of pitfalls that lay ahead full of dangers and horrors beyond imagining. As the first hints of fear had grasped him, Raamo had looked around him, searching the faces and the minds of those who stood with him on the high stage—the others who, with him, had begun the changes—to see if they, too, sensed the dangers.

He looked from face to face—from Neric to Genaa, to Hiro to D'ol Falla, and to the Erdlings, Kanna and

Herd—and he saw that they were worried and fearful, but also proud and joyous. And he saw that their fear was not the same as his.

He knew then that his fear arose, in part, from a strange vague beckoning that told him it was his task to find and confront a great danger. D'ol Falla had always insisted that he was meant to be a Spirit-messenger, a foreteller, but he had always doubted. Now this inner beckoning seemed to tell him he was destined to some purposing as yet far beyond his understanding, and he found himself resisting, not with doubt, but with terror. He did not know what he would be required to do, but he felt evil nearby and growing, like a brooding presence. He felt it to be deep-rooted and of great power, and he was terribly afraid that he was meant to seek it out and protect the children—and perhaps others as well—from its consuming darkness.

When the planning was accomplished, the talk had turned once more to uniforce and miracles, and the men and women of the Geets-kel, troubled and shaken by their contemplation of the days to come, had returned eagerly to the Joy they had discovered in their newfound faith. And it was then that Raamo had left the hall, removing his private fear and doubt from the midst of so much hopefulness.

At the doorway he turned for a moment to look back. The attention of the Geets-kel, clustered below the stage, as well as of those on the platform was centered on the children. Only Hiro and D'ol Falla stood apart, Hiro holding the tool-of-violence. He spoke to D'ol Falla, and she answered, and then she reached out and took the weapon carefully in both hands. And once again Raamo had felt an evil presence, moving through the bright Joy and trembling excitement, like the seeping waters of a dark river.

And so he had come to the farheights to look for Peace, and perhaps for some understanding of the beckoning—of what it was that had called to him and why. But even there, rocked in the swaying leaf-cushioned nid, and soothed by the enfolding cloud-softened sky, the fear remained unchanged, and still hidden.

Then at last, it came to him that if he were truly Spirit-summoned, it could not be without reason—and when the time came, he would understand what was needed and what was required of him. With the first warm drops of rain, a kind of Peace fell on him, and he drifted in it, tempted for a time to go on lying there all through the night. But he sat up instead, and as his leafy nid rocked wildly, he was suddenly aware that the fear had become bearable. It was not so much diminished, but more as if he, himself, had changed. As if he had made an accommodation so that the fear's space no longer crowded out hope and many other things as well.

He left the farheights and climbed downwards to where the thinning topgrowth left space for gliding. Shaking out the wing-panels of his shuba, he leaned forward into a glide. But here in the uninhabited forest there were no cleared glidepaths, and he was forced to turn and bank sharply. As he dropped lower, the dark quickly deepened, making such maneuvering more dangerous, and he was soon forced to land and continue by branchpath.

He was moving southward, towards Orbora, and had almost reached the boundaries of Temple Grove when he stopped suddenly and listened. Someone was ap-

11

proaching, below him and slightly to the south. Faint sounds reached his ears, the soft brush of feet on branchpath, the occasional snap of a broken twig, and now and then the cautious hiss of whispering voices. Dropping to his stomach, Raamo slid forward and peered over the edge of the branch.

Not far below him a small procession was making its way along a large branchpath. Of the six figures, four were heavily laden with portage baskets; and even in the semi-darkness, it was apparent that the other two were dressed in the shimmering white shubas of Ol-zhaan. The first was tall and thick bodied, his step slow and ponderous, while the other, who scurried beside him in stumbling haste, was short and formless as a tree tuber.

Clearly the large Ol-zhaan was D'ol Regle, and the short formless one, his ardent disciple, D'ol Salaat. The other four were, perhaps, servants from the palace of the novice-master. It seemed that D'ol Regle had, indeed, decided to flee to the open forest and live in exile.

Perhaps it was for the best, Raamo told himself. What good could come of his presence in Orbora? It would be only a continual reminder of what he had tried to do, and such a reminder would surely cause only fear and mind-pain. But when the novice-master and his followers had disappeared from sight in the thick untrimmed growth of the open forest, Raamo's fear did not go with them.

12

CHAPTER TWO

E arly the next morning, two people descended the rampway from Broadgrund
and slowly crossed the wide platform that
served as an entry way to the assembly hall of Orbora.
The great hall, built during the glorious early days of
the planet, was still unsurpassed—a monument to the
time when the creative genius of the Kindar was at its
height. Securely supported by two great grundbranches,
it appeared to be almost floating among masses of
greenery, its soaring arches and lacy screens blending
in perfect harmony with the surrounding forest. But its
wonders were lost on the man and woman who were
approaching it at that moment. Deep in conversation,
they spoke in tense urgent voices of matters that clearly
concerned them greatly. The woman was D'ol Falla,
and the man upon whose arm she was leaning was Hiro
D'anhk.

"It is indeed a pity," D'ol Falla was saying, "that so
much must be asked of you—such a great burden of
responsibility placed on you—when you have so recently returned from exile. I know you would much
prefer to be free to enjoy your reunion with Jorda and

13

with Genaa. But there is no one else among us who can speak to the Kindar as one of their own. Except for Kanna and Herd, who are Erdling and alien, we are all Ol-zhaan, and therefore tainted."

"But surely Neric will be able to earn their trust," Hiro said, "when they learn that it was he who began the search for the truth."

"Perhaps," D'ol Falla said, "but Neric is very young and inexperienced. I fear his certainty and his impulsiveness. In the days to come there may be great need to move slowly and with caution if we are to avoid disaster."

Hiro sighed deeply. "That is true," he said. "I will speak to the Kindar as you ask. But what would you have me say?"

"Tell them where you have been, and why. The rest will follow. I will speak first and tell them the truth concerning the past—of the true fate of the ancestral planet, and of the dispute that led to the banishment of the first exiles. And then, when the Kindar see you— when they see that you are still alive—they will be prepared to hear the truth concerning the Pash-shan."

"I don't know," Hiro said. "When they see me, they may be forced to accept the truth; but I am afraid that nothing can prepare them for it. How can you prepare a people to lose, in so short a time, not only their saints, the Ol-zhaan, but their demons as well? I'm afraid that they will not easily relinquish their fear of the Pash-shan."

They reached the doorway of the great hall then, and entering, they made their way down the long sloping aisle between the rows of tendril benches and mounted the curving rampway that led to the high stage. Soon

14

after, the others began to arrive. First the young Ol-zhaan—Raamo, Genaa and Neric—and with them the two Erdlings, dressed now in Kindar shubas, but still alien in their appearance, with their golden skin tones and dark, uncropped hair.

Genaa was glowing, and Neric's round eyes gleamed with eager anticipation; but Raamo's face was shadowed as if by sleeplessness or mind-pain. D'ol Falla would have questioned him, but the others were coming now, the Geets-kel, in groups of two or three. And not long after, the Kindar began to enter the great hall.

In contrast to the Geets-kel, who were tense and strained, the Kindar leaders were relaxed and at ease. Curious, perhaps, at the sudden summons, but entirely unaware of the shattering revelations that were soon to come. Dressed in richly ornamented shubas, many adorned with sashes of high office, they took their places on the tendril benches and addressed their attention to the high stage where the group of Ol-zhaan were seated. And with the Ol-zhaan, two Kindar—odd, swarthy people, groomed in an unlikely manner—possibly visitors from Farvald or one of the other more provincial cities.

But then D'ol Falla, the ancient and honored priest of the Vine, came forward and began to speak to them. Beginning bluntly, without the accustomed rituals of greeting between Ol-zhaan and Kindar, she began to tell them things they had never thought to hear.

The first part of the telling concerned the ancestral planet; and shocking though it was, it did not come as a complete surprise to many of the Kindar leaders. There were many among them who were learned men and women, clear-minded and curious, who had long

15

received the old legends and histories as truthful only in a symbolic way. In song and story, as well as on numberless tapestries and wall hangings, the ancestral planet had been depicted as a dimly distant fairyland, and the flight itself as a birdlike migration led by the shining figures of the legendary heroes, D'ol Wissen and D'ol Nesh-om. But although some suspected that the flight had been made on wings more substantial than those of a shuba, and that it had been undertaken for reasons more compelling than the promptings of the Spirit—they had no words to express their suspicions, and no desire to face their implications.

But now D'ol Falla stood before them telling them monstrous things about their ancestors and the fate of their ancestral planet, things that could only be described by using forbidden vernacularisms of the most vulgar sort—grossly obscene in their meanings and painfully embarrassing to hear spoken in a public gathering. But there was more, and worse, to come.

D'ol Falla spoke next concerning the first Ol-zhaan, the two great leaders, D'ol Wissen and D'ol Nesh-om, and how a disagreement had arisen between them concerning innocence and truth—D'ol Nesh-om insisting that the Kindar should know the truth concerning their heritage of violence and the tragic fate of their ancestors, and D'ol Wissen certain that only a carefully guarded and protected innocence could prevent a return to the violent patterns of the past.

"But then D'ol Nesh-om died," D'ol Falla told them, "and for a time D'ol Wissen prevailed, but he knew that there were some who still believed in the teachings of D'ol Nesh-om. D'ol Wissen feared that, after his death, those who opposed him would reverse his decisions. So at a great age, and feeling himself near death, he made use of his great skill in grunspreking to produce an enchanted and invulnerable barrier between earth and sky, and he imprisoned all who had opposed him below the Root."

An audible gasp of horror arose from many throats, and although it was unvoiced, it spoke clearly of a single thought.

"The Pash-shan?" D'ol Falla asked. "You are thinking that surely D'ol Wissen could not have knowingly sent humans to certain death at the hands of the Pash-shan? And indeed, he did not. He sent them only to a dark and endless banishment—because the Pash-shan do not exist and never have."

Speaking into a stunned silence, D'ol Falla went on to explain how the secret had been kept over the many years that followed. How even the Ol-zhaan were kept in ignorance concerning the true nature of the Pash-shan, except for a select and secret few who were chosen to become Geets-kel—a society dedicated to the maintenance of prisons, the prison in which the minds of the Kindar were held in bondage, as well as the great underground dungeon that confined the exiles, and the ever-growing number of their descendants.

"I, myself, have for many years been a Geets-kel, a prison-keeper," D'ol Falla said, "as have most of these others whom you see before you. But now you must learn why we will no longer be prison-keepers, and why many things will no longer be as they have been in Green-sky."

D'ol Falla turned then and summoned someone who came forward from the wings of the high stage and approached to stand beside her. It was—surely it could not be—Hiro D'anhk. Most of the Kindar leaders had known him well when, as Director of the Academy, he had been an honored scholar and a leader among them. His lean, well-favored face was still written in their memories, although he had been gone—dead—lost to the Pash-shan, more than two years before. And yet, he now stood before them—one more unbelievable fact out of many. But this fact appeared to be of flesh and blood.

"My old friends," the apparition was saying, "as you can see, I have not been dead these last two years, but only among the banished, and now, I think, you are beginning to understand where I have been and why."

Hiro went on speaking, and the Kindar sat before him, but some of them had ceased to listen. Standing above them on the platform, Raamo could feel the force of their denial, a cold tension, full of confusion and fear. In the second row an old man wearing the gray-green sash of a grund-master reached furtively into his waist pouch and, bending low, brought his hand quickly to his lips. Watching him, Raamo could almost taste the thick cloying sweetness of the Berry, and feel the soothing numbness that would soon flood the grund-master's mind, drowning his anxiety in calm clouds of oblivion.

Hiro had begun to speak of the Erdlings—the banished Kindar—and of how their increasing numbers had doomed them to constant hunger and, if help did not come soon, to death by starvation. Calling forward the two Erdlings, Kanna and Herd Eld, Hiro gave their names and had them each speak briefly to the audience. In their unfamiliar accents, slow and slurring, they spoke

18

of how they had come as representatives, to seek first food and eventually freedom for their people.

The Kindar listened in total silence. Raamo could pense a strange dark confusion, touched here and there with revulsion—as if there were some who saw these thin alien humans as monsters in disguise—as if they could not possibly be other than monstrous, since they had admittedly come from below the Root.

"I would ask a question, Hiro D'anhk, if it is you, indeed, returned to us from the dead." It was Ruulba D'arsh who spoke, the City-master of Orbora, and at one time a close friend of Hiro. "I would ask how it is that these Ol-zhaan—these who have called themselves the Geets-kel—have decided to speak out now, after so many years of silence?"

Hiro raised his arms in the embracing gesture used at the meeting of intimate friends. "Greetings, old friend," he said, smiling. "It is like you, Ruulba, to remain clear-headed at a time of confusion, and to come forward with questions that need asking. The answer to your question can be shown as well as told."

Turning, Hiro motioned Raamo, Neric, and Genaa to come forward and stand beside him. "The answer to Ruulba's question stands here before you," Hiro told the Kindar leaders. "These three young Ol-zhaan, whom you have known as D'ol Neric, D'ol Raamo, and D'ol Genaa, discovered the secret of the Geets-kel, and it was their actions that brought about this meeting—this moment when the truth is given back to all the people of Green-sky. It was Neric who first began to suspect the truth," Hiro said, putting his arm across Neric's shoulders and leading him forward. A sharp gasp arose from the audience, and Hiro realized that he had made a mistake. There would be time later to question old traditions and taboos, such as the use of the respectful title D'ol and the taboo against physical contact between Ol-zhaan and Kindar. There were more urgent changes to be accepted—and shock enough in the acceptance.

Stepping back to a respectful distance, he gestured to Raamo. "And it was the Spirit-gifts of the novice Ol-zhaan, D'ol Raamo, that helped to verify D'ol Neric's suspicions."

There was pride in Hiro's voice as he finally gestured towards his beautiful daughter. "And it was my daughter, Genaa—D'ol Genaa—who joined them when she learned that my disappearance had been the work, not of the Pash-shan, but of the Geets-kel."

How much to tell the Kindar on that first day of truth had been carefully considered, and it had been decided that it would be best to say as little as possible about the role played by D'ol Regle—about his incredible threat, and how near he had come to making use of the tool-of-violence. There would be time enough later for the Kindar to learn of such great evil so narrowly escaped. So Hiro finished his story simply by saying that the three young Ol-zhaan had been joined by D'ol Falla, and together they had finally been able to convince the Ol-zhaan that the truth must be told, and thus they had all come today, to stand before the Kindar and share in the telling.

It seemed to Raamo that Hiro's words were falling into a great emptiness. There was no response at all. The Kindar leaders sat before him, their eyes on his face, but there were no comments of understanding and approval, nor any of doubt and denial. There was only a distance that seemed to grow constantly greater and more dense.

D'ol Falla turned to Raamo, but he only shook his

21

head, and she knew that he pensed nothing more than she—a kind of retreat, a pulling back and turning away that grew stronger and more desperate with every moment that passed.

Hiro was still speaking, telling the Kindar of the decision that had been made to form a council, a Joined Council, made up of leaders from the Erdling community as well as from the Kindar. This council would consider the problems involved in uniting the two societies, and the best possible solutions.

"All of you who were asked to be present today are leaders, men and women of high honor and proven ability," Hiro told the silent Kindar. "And we will need your help in the days that lie ahead. Who among you will come forward now to serve on the Joined Council and lend your strength and wisdom to the building of a new Green-sky—a Green-sky of freedom and truth?"

There was movement then, among those who listened, as the Kindar let their eyes fall and turned their faces away from Hiro's entreaty. Stepping to the edge of the platform, Hiro spoke directly to some who had been well known to him, a few of them even since his youth hall days.

"Guraa, Savaan, Ruulba," he said, "will you not join us? Will you not offer your services to the Council and to all Green-sky? We will need such talents as yours desperately in the days ahead."

There followed a long and painful waiting, and at last D'ol Falla came to stand beside Hiro and speak again to the assembly.

"Honored leaders and scholars," she said. "Perhaps we ask too much, too suddenly. It is understandable that there must be time to consider so great a commitment.

22

But in the meantime there is another matter—a smaller commitment, but one that must be undertaken without delay. I am speaking of providing food for the Erdlings. We will need help from those of you who are experienced in organizing and directing projects that require the efforts of large numbers of Kindar. We will need guild-masters and grund-leaders, who can provide teams of workers to carry large quantities of food from the public warehouses down to the forest floor where they can be transferred to the tunnel openings that lie near the underground city of Erda."

The result of D'ol Falla's request was near panic. It had seemed to her that the Kindar's obvious reluctance to assume the awful responsibility of leadership at a time of such crisis might be lessened if the task to be accomplished was simpler and more limited. But she had not taken into account the great power of old fears —of fears implanted in infancy and carefully nurtured. The faces that turned upwards towards D'ol Falla as she spoke were stiff with shock, and everywhere eyes gleamed with unreasoned fear.

D'ol Falla knew what she had done even before Raamo stood beside her and whispered in her ear. "They are frightened, D'ol Falla," he said. "They fear the forest floor, and the dark tunnels and those who dwell below the Root."

"They don't believe what we have told them?" D'ol Falla asked.

"I think they believe," Raamo said. "They think 'Erdling,' but they still feel 'Pash-shan'."

An old woman, a guild-master, struggled to her feet and rushed blindly out of the assembly hall, and others began to stir furtively, as if gathering themselves for a

23

quick retreat. It was only too clear that something had to be done and quickly. It was D'ol Falla who made the decision.

"Wait," she cried. "Stop and listen. There is more. You have heard many strange and terrible things, and you are fearful and confused. But there is more, and if you will listen, you will be greatly comforted."

So, on impulse and in desperation, D'ol Falla changed the decision to say nothing, on that first day, of the children and D'ol Regle. Turning to the others on the high stage, she said urgently, "I am afraid that all is lost, unless—the miracle—uniforce? . . ." and the others nodded in agreement, except for Raamo, who held out his hands to D'ol Falla and cried, "Wait, wait!"

But D'ol Falla did not hear him, or if she did, she felt she could not wait. So she turned back to the Kindar and began to tell them the story of the two children —who they were and how they had come to live and play together—and of how D'ol Regle, the novice-master, had stolen them to hold them hostage in order to force the rebels to give up their plans to take the truth to the people.

She told the story well, and it soon became apparent that the Kindar were listening. They continued to listen as she described the tool-of-violence, the ancient artifact brought to Green-sky from the ancestral planet, and the terrible use that D'ol Regle had threatened to make of it if his orders were not obeyed.

She told of her own plea to Raamo for a foretelling that would show them how to meet D'ol Regle's threat, and how the prophecy had come to him in the form of a song—a song that they had all known as children. Then, as Raamo had sung the song, the bound and helpless

24

children had stretched forth their hands and released a great power—a power that raised the ancient weapon from the table and sent it drifting lightly as a mist-borne petal, surrounding it with a flowing force, which seemed to blur and soften its deadly form and meaning.

Finally D'ol Falla spoke of faith—of the faith that had returned to the Geets-kel and caused them to forget their fears and to pledge themselves to the cause of the Rejoyning. And of Nesh-om's faith, which had proclaimed the possibility of a world where no hand would be lifted except to offer Love and Joy.

The silence returned when D'ol Falla ceased to speak, but it was not the same silence as before. The fear was still there and the confusion, but now there was also an openness, a seeking. After a long time, someone spoke. A woman, an instructor at the academy, rose to her feet and asked to see the children, and immediately many others repeated her request.

"The children," the Kindar were saying. "Show us the children."

So Herd Eld left the hall and went hastily to fetch his daughter, Teera, and Pomma D'ok. While he was gone, those who remained behind in the assembly hall waited in a breathless hush, so delicately balanced on the edge of hysteria that no one on the platform dared to speak for fear the sound of his voice might be the trigger to chaos. But the stillness held and, at last, Herd returned with the children.

Raamo waited for their arrival in a state of great anxiety. He could not understand his apprehension. Clearly, the story of the children had brought about a good change in the people. But when, at last, the children arrived and were led out onto the stage, it seemed

25

to him that his fears were justified, although he could not have said why.

As Herd Eld led them out onto the great platform, the children clung to his hands, their heads drooping. Raamo could see that Pomma's blue-green eyes were wide with fear, and her fragile paleness made her seem almost a ghost child, formed of mist and shadow. Even Teera's rich, warm beauty seemed dulled and faded, and she ducked her head so that her long dark hair shielded her face from the staring eyes of the Kindar leaders.

Slowly Herd led the children forward to the edge of the platform and, pushing them gently ahead of him, he stepped back, leaving them standing alone. For a moment they stood stiffly, their eyes downcast. Then Pomma's hand groped for Teera's, and suddenly they were clinging together, as children will, for strength and comfort.

And that was all. There was no return of uniforce. No miraculous reversal of the laws of nature. Nothing at all happened—except that suddenly everything had changed. The great warm wave that swept through the assembly hall carried fear and doubt before it, and brought many of the Kindar leaders forward to pledge their support and to volunteer their services as members of the Joined Council. There were even two or three who, wild-eyed with terror at their own daring, offered to take part in the carrying of food to the forest floor.

For the moment Raamo, too, was caught up in that great warm wave, so that, for a time, he forgot the inner voice that warned him to protect Pomma and Teera from something that he did not understand.

CHAPTER THREE

W hen the story of the children and the miraculous reappearance of uni-force had turned the Kindar leaders back from the edge of despair, it had seemed to the Rejoyners that a great danger had been safely passed. But they were soon to discover that the days that followed would bring one dangerous crisis after another in a seemingly endless procession. It was on the second day that the truth was taken to the Ol-zhaan, and another crisis arose—one of perhaps even greater peril.

This time the meeting was held in the Temple Hall in the grove of the Ol-zhaan. Messengers had been sent to the outlying cities, and all the Ol-zhaan in Green-sky were present—more than one hundred white-clad figures, men and women who varied greatly in age and appearance, but who were strangely alike in subtle ways that spoke of long familiarity with honor, privilege, and power. But by then, by that second morning, rumors had already started to fly, and this time the meeting began in an atmosphere that was heavy with apprehension.

Once again most of the speaking was done by Hiro

and D'ol Falla, but since the true history of the ancestral planet was known to all Ol-zhaan, the telling began with the secrets of the Geets-kel—those that concerned the true nature of the Pash-shan, the meaning of the name Erdling, and the need to bring justice and freedom to those who bore that name.

Just as there had been with the Kindar, there was at the beginning a shocked disbelief, but the reaction that followed was not at all the same. Instead of fearful retreat, there was anger, and a kind of bitter outrage. It was unthinkable to Ol-zhaan that they had been kept in ignorance, betrayed by their own kind—that a select few among their fellows had taken it on themselves to keep the truth from all the rest as if they were ignorant and untrustworthy children. There were many who spoke out in righteous anger, and a few who spoke not only of the pain of their betrayal, but of their horror at the greater betrayal—the generations of Kindar unjustly imprisoned.

The fear did not come until later when the first shock was over and the Ol-zhaan had turned their minds to solutions—and had begun to realize their own dilemma. If the Erdlings were freed, the Kindar would, of course, learn the truth—and not only the truth concerning the Pash-shan but other truths as well. They would learn the facts concerning their tragic heritage, and perhaps, most disillusioning of all, they would soon discover that for many generations the skills of the Spirit had been as rare among the Ol-zhaan as among the Kindar themselves. The Ol-zhaan saw that not only the deceits of the Geets-kel, but their own deceits as well, must be exposed. And it was then that D'ol Falla's wisdom became apparent, when she had insisted that the truth be taken first to the Kindar, so that there could be no turning back.

It was D'ol Ruuro, an orchard protector, who spoke first of waiting. "I would not have it thought," he told the assembly, "that I condone what these—these Geetskel, as they call themselves—have done. Nor that I would not wish to undo the evil done to the exiles. But we must think of the welfare of the Kindar. We must think what it will do to our own Kindar to be stripped so suddenly of all that they revere and honor. Surely we must take great pains to move slowly and carefully . . ."

Before D'ol Ruuro's voice had died away, there were others who began to echo him, and many were eager to agree. But then D'ol Falla told them of what had already been done, of the assembling of the Kindar leaders on the day before.

The Ol-zhaan saw at once that there could be no turning back, and the great hall was swept with such fear and anger that Raamo closed his mind against the dark waves, which threatened to drown his reason. Still standing with the other Rejoyners before the altar, he retreated into himself, so that he did not realize at once that the story of the rebirth of uniforce was being used again to bring about acceptance and reconciliation. It was not until much later that he sensed a change and knew it resulted from a great surge of faith.

On the third day the newly appointed Kindar members of what would be the Joined Council met and many changes were begun. A series of public meetings were arranged to take the truth, little by little, to all the members of Kindar society. The first transport crew was formed to begin the distribution of food to the

29

Erdlings. And a delegation was appointed to visit Erda and confer with the Erdling leaders.

Hiro D'anhk, along with the Erdling, Herd Eld, was chosen to lead the delegation to Erda. Hiro accepted the task with great reluctance. He had, after all, been reunited with his family for only a few days. But even more important, he saw the dangers threatening all the people of Green-sky, and the need for confident leadership. When so much had occurred in three short days, who could say what might take place in three more, and Hiro could not help feeling extremely anxious about leaving Orbora at such a time of crisis.

However, the mission of the delegation to Erda was one of great delicacy and its outcome would be of fateful importance. Since he had lived in Erda and had already earned the respect and trust of the Erdlings, he was well suited to the task. Under his guidance the Kindar leaders would have to be led from the secret opening in the Root to the Center. The members of the Erdling Council would have to be contacted and a number of them chosen to serve on the Joined Council and persuaded to accompany the delegation on its return to Orbora. But most difficult and delicate of all, the Erdling Council would have to be persuaded that the secret of the opening in the Root would have to be kept a little longer—that the Erdling people should remain below the Root until the Joined Council could meet, and a safe and orderly process of resettlement could be worked out. So Hiro D'anhk returned to Erda, accompanied by Herd Eld and six Kindar Councilmen, while in the city of Orbora, great changes continued to take place with every day that passed.

It was Neric and Genaa who organized and led the

30

first of the public meetings to which the common people of Orbora were summoned. On the first day of the meetings, the people listened in silence, their faces rigid with fear and denial, but during later assemblies the fear seemed to grow less. Many of the Kindar seemed to be responding to the shocking revelations with a calm acceptance. The young leaders were heartened until they realized what was happening—after the first day, the summoned Kindar were forewarned by rumor and they came prepared, fortified against terror by large quantities of the Sacred Berry.

Both Neric and Genaa were greatly disturbed. "Who knows," Neric demanded, "what they understood of all that they were told. Who knows how much they even heard. Words fall like birdsong on the ears of Berry-dreamers—a soothing sound but without meaning. I doubt if our assemblies have served any purpose at all."

But Genaa was more hopeful. "I'm not sure," she told Neric, "but I think that most of them have heard. Remember how they reacted to the story of the children."

It was true, Neric conceded. No matter how terror stricken or how far gone in Berry-dreaming, the story of the children seemed to bring hope and life to the faces of the Kindar.

"I for one," he told Genaa, "can see nothing but good in the people's faith in the children. 'I might almost be tempted to think that our saintly Raamo was human enough to be jealous, except that he is just as much opposed to our using the people's faith in him, as seer and prophet."

"I know," Genaa said. "I can't understand it. I have

asked him many times to explain it to me, but he seems unable to give me a logical answer."

Neric nodded. "Only yesterday I said to him, 'It is the truth, Raamo. What we tell the people about the children is the truth. And are we not committed to the giving of truth?' And he answered, 'Yes, we must give them the truth, but not great truths. Great truths are dangerous gifts.' "

"What does that mean?" Genaa asked.

"I don't know. When I asked him to explain, he only frowned thoughtfully and admitted that he didn't know." Frowning thoughtfully, Neric made his voice soft and slow and said, " 'I—I don't know, I don't know what it means—but I think it is true.' "

They laughed together, and Genaa said, "Dear Raamo. What is to be done with him?"

And so they continued to talk to the people about the children, and, in truth, they no longer had a choice in the matter. Rumor had already spread the story to every part of Green-sky, so that there were always those, in even the most silent group of Kindar, who asked to have it told. The telling was done either by Neric or Genaa, or even at times by D'ol Birta, who, as an Ol-zhaan had been chief counselor to the Gardens of Orbora, and who was now an ardent supporter of the Rejoyning.

Whoever did the telling, the results were much the same. The Kindar listened eagerly to the story of the delicate, ailing Kindar child and how she began to share her life with the darkly beautiful daughter of Erdlings, of how together the two relearned the Spirit-skills of infancy and then, when great evil threatened, brought back to Green-sky the almost forgotten power

32

of united Spirit-force. Each time, when the telling was over, where there had been fear and apathy, there was faith and hope.

While Neric and Genaa went daily to the Kindar assemblies, Raamo and D'ol Falla remained in the Temple Grove. It was their task to form the first transport crews that would carry food to the Erdling tunnels from the orchards and public warehouses. The decision to use Ol-zhaan volunteers to man the first food caravans had been partly politic and partly a matter of necessity. It was to be a gesture of humility and concern on the part of the Ol-zhaan that might begin to erase prejudices born of generations of fear and hatred. But still, it was also a necessity, because very few of the Kindar were as yet able to face a journey to the forbidden forest floor.

In other gatherings the Ol-zhaan met to discuss the changes that lay ahead: the role they would play in those changes, and the ways their own lives would be affected. Torn from positions of honor and power, they were soon to be reduced to common humanity—or perhaps much worse. They felt themselves to be victims: victims of the Geet-kel's deceit, of the Kindar's disenchantment, and, most frightening of all, of the Erdling's pent-up hatred. There were some who saw flight as the only answer. Among those was D'ol Povaal, a high ranked guild-priest.

"We will be forced to flee, in the end," D'ol Povaal repeatedly told his fellow Ol-zhaan, "one by one, and in terror. Unless we follow the example of D'ol Regle and go quickly at a time of our own choosing. Let us go now, all of us together, into the open forest where, banded together we can establish a new city. A city of Ol-zhaan, separate and apart, and therefore free from

33

the unjust persecution that will be our lot now in all the seven cities."

There were some who agreed with the guild-priest, but many others who did not. Some disagreed for practical reasons. There were none among the Ol-zhaan who were practiced in the skills necessary to daily life. None who could weave shubas or carve furniture, prepare food or shape walls and roofs of frond and tendril. There were many who, from lack of practice, had even forgotten how to weave a nid.

Others resisted flight for reasons of conscience, whatever their personal fate might be. A few were too despairing to plan any action at all, and there were some who were fully committed to goals of the Rejoyning, and who wished to stay that they might serve those goals in whatever way possible. Calling themselves the Ny-zhaan, this latter group listened earnestly to the advice of D'ol Falla, regarded Raamo with reverent awe, and spoke constantly of the miracle of the sacred children. Within the space of ten days' time, many of these Ny-zhaan had discarded their white shubas and, leaving the Temple Grove, had begun to move into the guild homes and youth halls of the city.

D'ol Falla heartily approved of the actions of the Ny-zhaan. It was right and fair, she said, that the Temple Grove should belong to all the Kindar—its temples open to all and its palaces transformed into youth halls or residences. But for the time, only one Kindar family came to live within the sacred grove, and they came for special and urgent reasons. They were Raamo's family, Hearba and Valdo D'ok and his sister Pomma, who had found it impossible to stay in the D'ok nid-place. With them came the Erdling family of Teera Eld.

The two families had been sharing the D'ok nid-place, but as the story of the miraculous reappearance of uni-force spread over Green-sky, they found that they were living in a shrine, a place of pilgrimage. Daily the wide branchpath on each side of their nid-place was packed with people waiting to get a glimpse of the inhabitants, and in particular, of Teera and Pomma. With each day the wild enthusiasm of the crowd at the slightest glimpse of the children became more and more uncontrollable. All of the immense faith and trust, which had for so long been placed in the Ol-zhaan, seemed to have been turned towards the children. And the faith was made all the more intense by the frightening uncertainties of the future. The children were a symbol of hope and of Spirit-power. And the Kindar daily demonstrated their faith in the traditional ways—by the singing and shouting and ritual gesturing, which had, for generations, greeted the objects of their devotion.

At last, under cover of rain and darkness, the two families were smuggled out of the D'ok nid-place and taken to the Vine Palace; and there they remained.

CHAPTER FOUR

W hen the first delegation returned to Orbora after four days below the Root, they brought with them four Erdling Councilors. Among them was the old man, Kir Oblan, who had long been a respected leader in Erda, and three others of similar ability and renown. They brought with them, also, a certain amount of optimism and enthusiasm. The Kindar delegates, who had started out upon their mission with grave doubts and fears, had been delighted, and greatly relieved, at the humanity of the Erdlings. They had found the Erdling Council to be friendly and cooperative.

An agreement had quickly been made. If the transfer of food supplies to Erda could begin quickly, the Erdling Councilers would agree to keep the secret of the opening in the Root until after the Joined Council had had time to make careful and thorough preparations for the reunion of the two societies. Yet only a few days after their return to Orbora, during the second meeting of the Joined Council, a breathless messenger appeared suddenly in the assembly hall and announced that large numbers of Erdlings had been seen above the Root—walking freely on the forest floor.

The Kindar egg-gatherer who first saw the Erdlings was too frightened to approach them, but if he had he would have noticed that one was a child of no more than nine years, a boy with wide-set gray eyes and broad sturdy shoulders. The boy was Charn Arnd, a cavern-kin and onetime playmate of Teera Eld. Except for Teera, herself, Charn had become the first Erdling child to stand above the Root.

Charn had been amazed and delighted and a little chagrined when he first learned the facts about Teera's whereabouts.

"She did it," he had told Raula Sarp, who with Charn had been a favorite playmate of Teera. "She was always saying she was going to live in the forest someday. And she really did it. She went up there and turned into a Kindar. I still don't believe it."

Quite suddenly, there had come to be a large number of things in Charn's world that were very hard to believe. When Teera had disappeared, he had grieved for her truly and deeply for many days. But then, just as he was beginning to forget his grief, he was told that Teera was alive. The fact that Teera was alive, however, was a secret he must not tell, and where she was and why, was a secret that he could not yet be told. Charn was not fond of secrets of either kind.

From that time on, unbelievable things began to happen, one after another, and it became obvious to Charn that people he knew well, members of his clan, were very much involved in these strange new things that were happening in Erda. And it was also very obvious to him that it was quite unfair that he, himself, was so little involved, with nothing more to do than to wait.

Therefore, when the Kindar visitors left the Center,

Charn followed along, with hundreds of other curious Erdlings. He followed the procession to a large outlying cavern where, after the Kindar and Erdling Councilors and their escorts had entered a tunnel, guards had been posted and no one was allowed to go farther. But Charn did not give up easily.

As the crowd gradually thinned, Charn worked his way over to the tunnel entrance. There he sat down against a rock formation to rest, and after a while he heard one of the guards talking to a small group of people. The guard was saying that he had overheard the Kindar speaking of a passageway through the Root, and that he was going to try to find it—the next time he was on duty, in two days time.

So Charn had come back two days later, to find that the guard had told his secret to quite a few more people. So many, that when they all started out on their search, they scarcely seemed to notice or care that a small extra person had joined the party. Trailing behind the group for fear that he would be noticed and sent back, he had been in a state of near-exhaustion by the time the opening was finally found. And then he had come very close to being left behind in the tunnel. Lifting and boosting each other, most of the members of the party had scrambled out, completely ignoring Charn and his polite requests for assistance. Finally, when the last man was being lifted out, Charn stopped being polite and began to yell as if he were being killed. And then the guard had seen him. Kneeling at the edge of the hole, he peered down at Charn with frowning impatience.

"Should just leave you down there," he muttered as he reached down for Charn's hands. "No business being here at all. Don't suppose you have a token or two about you?"

"No," Charn sniffed as he scrambled to his feet on the forest floor. "I don't have any tokens."

The guard shrugged. "Thought not. The fee was ten tokens. That's what all the others paid me. Sure you don't have even one token?"

When Charn shook his head, the guard frowned so fiercely that for a moment Charn thought that he was about to be thrown back down the hole. But then the guard went off, still muttering, and Charn was left alone—above the Root.

It was green and high and bright. Later that was all he could think to say when Raula questioned him.

"Green and high and bright," she shouted at him finally. "I know it's green and high and bright. What else was it like. Tell me."

There was more, of course, to tell. But Charn had been so dazzled—so excited and more than a little frightened—that it had all swirled together in his mind like a great shining confusion. There was bigness; space that went up and up and up without end, enormous pillars that were the start of grundtrees, and shining, shimmering things of all colors that sprang up around him from the earth. He was just beginning to sort it all out in his mind when the brightness went away and darkness began. Darkness like an unlit tunnel, except that the darkness above the Root was wet and full of sound and movement.

He had been very frightened, so when some of the others passed him on their way back to the opening in the Root, he followed them, and returned to Erda.

And two days later, when Raula had talked him into returning and taking her, they found that a new and very large party of guards had been posted and everyone was being turned away.

But new things continued to happen. There soon began to be more food on the table-stones of Erda. Only a little more at first, and at times, strange things that Charn had never before tasted and wouldn't have liked at all, except that he was so hungry. And then, before long, there was talk of moving above the Root.

Charn wasn't at all sure he wanted to, at first. It seemed to him that if you went to live above the Root, it would be very tiring to have to come so far every time you wanted to visit the people and places you knew best. But the grown-ups of the clan talked constantly of moving, although some of them were against it because it was still forbidden by the Council.

The guards had been removed, however, since most of them seemed to have been encouraging instead of preventing the traffic to the forest floor. And there were many in Erda who took the rulings of the Councils as a child takes the advice of parents—as well meant, but not necessarily binding.

The first surface cities were already springing up on the forest floor. Built for the most part in makeshift fashion and of odd combinations of materials, they were inhabited, some said, by light-headed young people who cared little for Council law and less for responsibility to their clans and places of service. But although Charn's father sometimes agreed with those who spoke against the first surface dwellers, he still talked constantly about moving above the Root—and soon, very soon.

"We'll wait for the Council to lift the forbiddance," he said, "if the wait is not too much longer. But they should understand that we have had too much of waiting and of patience—generations too much."

"Who are they, father?" Charn asked.

"The Ol-zhaan," Prelf said.

"They are saying that there are no more Ol-zhaan," Charn's mother said. "They say there is no difference now between Ol-zhaan and Kindar."

"We'll see. Perhaps they have changed. But it seems to me that they could not have changed so quickly. Can an Ol-zhaan become a Kindar simply by changing the color of his shuba?"

Nevertheless, they remained in the cavern until they heard about the Root. They thought at first it was only a rumor—there had been so many rumors—but it soon became apparent that it was really true. The Root was truly withering! After being invulnerable for hundreds of years, the Root appeared to be quite suddenly losing its resistance to fire and steel, and new openings were being made in many places. Soon after the rumors began, Charn's father went out to see for himself; and when he came back to the cavern, he began to make preparations to leave the clan and move to the forest floor.

"But why?" Charn asked. "If we're going to leave Erda, why can't we move up into the grunds? Why can't we go to live in Orbora, like Teera, and wear shubas and glide and weave our nids from tendril like the Kindar do?"

"We will, we will," Prelf said, grabbing Charn and hugging him tightly. "We will someday. But it may be a long time from now. In the meantime, we can at least live in freedom—above the Root."

"But why will it be a long time before we can live high up like the Kindar?"

"Because there are no nid-places for us yet or shubas

for us to wear. And it would be dangerous to try to live in the heights before we have all learned to glide. There are your little brothers to think about, Charn. They are too young to realize the danger, and they would have to be watched constantly until they learned to glide."

"But what about the Kindar children?"

"They are watched very carefully until they are two years old and can be sent to the Gardens to learn to glide. And even so, some of them fall, as you know. The Councilors have said that there are nid-places being built for Erdling families as well as special Gardens for our children, but it will take a great deal of time before they are ready. In the meantime we can at least live in light and freedom."

So Charn went to live in the surface city called Upper Erda, and he soon grew used to the bright days of endless openness, and the close confinement of a tiny crowded nid-place during the long rain-wet nights. But sometimes he was lonely for the cavern and his old playmates. It was Teera he missed most. He longed to see her, but he knew he would probably never play with her again.

Something very strange had happened to Teera, something that Charn found hard to understand. People spoke of Teera now in solemn voices, like the voice of old Vatar when he was telling all the people about the Spirit. Charn knew all the stories by heart—all the things they were saying about Teera. About how Teera and a Kindar girl called Pomma had learned to do uniforce just as it had been done in the early days, and how it was because of what Teera had done that the Ol-zhaan had agreed to the freeing of the Erdlings.

It wasn't that Charn couldn't understand what people were saying. It was just that he couldn't make his image of the holy child of the stories seem anything like his memories of his noisy, fun-loving clan-sibling. He thought about it often and wondered. If he ever saw Teera again, would he recognize her, or would she look entirely different? Would she still like to play—now that she was holy? And did she like gliding and being a Kindar as much as she had always thought she would?

Charn would have been very puzzled if he had known that Teera still had not learned to glide. And he would have been amazed if he had been told that Teera's life in Green-sky had been, from the beginning, the life of a prisoner. Even now, when she was famous and holy and the object of boundless adoration, she still lived as a prisoner. Teera, herself, found it hard to understand.

At first, of course, she had been kept hidden in the D'ok nid-place because of the danger from the Geets-kel. Then there had been a real prison, while she and Pomma were held hostage by D'ol Regle. That much was easily understood. What was much harder to understand was why—now that there were no more Geets-kel, and she and Pomma were loved and honored by every-one—she was still kept prisoner.

The prison, of course, was large and beautiful. All the great halls and chambers, the latticed passageways and hanging rampways of the enormous palace were theirs to play in and explore. But there were some things that Teera wanted very much to do that could not be done inside the walls of a palace, no matter how large and beautiful.

She wanted to attend a Garden with other children. She wanted to explore the outer forest beyond the city.

She wanted to return to Erda, at least briefly, to see old friends and cavern-kin. Most of all, she wanted to learn to glide. And there was one other very important thing that Teera wanted, a simple thing, that now seemed strangely impossible. That was the chance to be with Pomma again.

It was not that she didn't see Pomma often. They were together daily, but seldom by themselves. The Vine Palace was usually full of people. And on the rare occasions when they were alone together, things were somehow not quite the same.

There were new games—fantasies of parades and processions and assemblies. The playing was grand and glorious and very exciting, but sometimes, afterwards, Teera felt tense and uneasy. Several times she and Pomma resolved not to play such games again. But their old games were not as they had been, and so they returned to the games of glory and honor. The glory and honor were hard to forget, and harder to understand.

Once, when they were alone in the hall of food-taking waiting for the others to arrive, they talked about it. A serving woman came into the room to leave a platter of pan-fruit; and when she saw that Pomma and Teera were there, she came up to them and held out her left hand in a gesture that signified a request for the blessing of Spirit-power. After she had gone, they had looked at each other strangely, and a part of the strangeness was shame.

"It's like we were Ol-zhaan," Pomma said. "Like all the people think we are wise and powerful."

"And holy," Teera said. "They call us holy."

Pomma nodded, her lips tucked in a strange, unsteady smile. Curious, Teera tried to pense what lay behind the

44

smile, but Pomma was mind-blocking. Teera sighed. They had seldom blocked with each other in the days before . . .

"I wonder," Pomma said. "I just wonder why?"

"Well, because of the uniforce, of course," Teera said bluntly.

"I know!" Pomma sounded impatient. "But why is uniforce so—so important?"

Teera only shrugged. She was feeling oddly resentful, without really knowing why, except that Pomma ought to know that all this talk was making her uncomfortable.

Then D'ol Falla entered and, in relief, Teera ran and threw her arms around the tiny old woman so hard she almost fell. Together they went back to Pomma, and then D'ol Falla hugged them both, and Teera was somewhat comforted by the strength of her love for them.

Cuddling against D'ol Falla, Pomma asked. "Why is uniforce so important, D'ol Falla? It's only moving things. Why does it make so much difference?"

"It's not the moving that is important," D'ol Falla told them. "It's the joining together of mind-force—the great growth of power that happens when Spirit-forces unite.

"In the early days, the power of uniforce was used in many ways. In healing, in grunspreking, in kiniporting. Seemingly impossible things were done with uniforce. For a time it seemed possible that it would provide solutions to many problems. There were even some who had begun attempts to store the energy of uniforce for later use, just as the Erdlings now use the stored energy of the black stone.

"There were problems of control, but even so uniforce became a symbol of the future—of progress and hope

45

and limitless possibilities. Then, gradually, it disappeared. So to see it return, as it did, and when it did—for the Rejoyning—was proof and vindication, and for all Green-sky it was the renewal of a legendary promise. There are some who think now that it is our only hope."

Teera did not understand all that D'ol Falla said, but it was clear that uniforce was much more than they had thought.

Pomma was still asking questions. "Will we have to? . . . Will they want us to do it again? To show them? To show all the people?" Her face was tight with anxiety, and Teera was quite certain that D'ol Falla would be able to guess what lay behind the question.

"There have been many requests," she said. And then, very gently, "Do you want to? Do you want to show the people uniforce?"

"No," they said, together.

"Then I think you will not have to. Unless—"

"Unless what?" Teera asked.

"I think you will not have to," D'ol Falla repeated.

But Teera remembered that D'ol Falla had said, "unless."

CHAPTER FIVE

With a morning's duties behind him and a free half-day ahead, Neric was on his way home to his nid-place in the Stargrund Youth Hall. The branchways were unusually crowded, and Neric pushed his way between silk-clad bodies with poorly concealed impatience. Near Broadtrunk, a passerby staggered as Neric brushed roughly against him, and then, noting the seal of office on Neric's chest, stepped hastily aside.

"Your pardon, Councilor."

"Your pardon," Neric replied and hurried on. If he was impatient, it was not without reason. Four hours at a Citizen's Senate in Freevald would undoubtedly have exhausted the patience of D'ol Nesh-om, himself. The Senates had been established to allow all the people of Green-sky, both Erdling and Kindar, to take part in solving the problems of the Rejoyning—to provide a place where suggestions could be made and progress reported. But the morning's session in Freevald, the newest of the surface cities, had been no more than an outpouring of complaints. The report that Neric would take to the Council would be, once again, a dreary listing of grievances, dissatisfactions and impatient requests.

Neric sighed. He had grown to dread assignment to the Senate meetings, but he supposed they were necessary. Hiro insisted that it was by constant coping with endless small dissatisfactions that disaster had been prevented time and time again, in the six months that had passed since the Rejoyning began.

He looked up to see that he was approaching a large crowd, gathered around the platform of a newsinger, and just as he began to wonder why so many people were listening, a quavering gasp arose from the mass of people. The newsinger's voice had just died away, but now it rose again, high-pitched and clearly agitated.

"Wassou was taken to the healing chambers in Grand-grund, and the Erdling—" here the newsinger paused as if in search of a permissable word, "—the Erdling injurers have not been seen since."

Reaching the platform, Neric gained the newsinger's attention by pulling sharply on the wing-panel of his shuba. "Tell me what has happened," he said. "I am a Councilor. If this matter has not been taken to the Council, it should be, and quickly. Is it the old man who was called D'ol Wassou who was injured?"

"Yes, Councilor. It was the Wassou who was an Ol-zhaan and Geets-kel before the Rejoyning. If you will release my shuba, I was about to begin the singing of it again, from the beginning."

So, shaking with impatience and anxiety, Neric was forced to listen to the lengthy and stylized account of the attack as it was slowly presented in the song-story of the newsinger. When the telling was finished, at last, Neric went immediately to the nid-place of Hiro D'anhk, the Chief Mediator of the Council, and soon afterwards he was again on his way to the Youth Hall. There, he would have time to eat and rest briefly, and then, having notified Genaa and Raamo, he would report back to the emergency meeting of the Council.

When he reached the Stargrund Youth Hall, Neric found that Raamo was not there. Genaa, however was in her chamber. Although it was midday, she was in her nid and apparently sound asleep. She awoke with obvious reluctance. As she listened to Neric's news, she shook her head violently from time to time, as if to convince herself that she had indeed awakened, and that what she was hearing was not part of some frightful dream.

"It must have been the Nekom," Neric told her. "Kir Oblan warned us of them when we were in Erda, and he has also spoken of them before the Council. You remember how their leader, the man called Axon Befal, tried to rouse the people against us and all Ol-zhaan."

"Yes," Genaa said. "I remember."

"Oblan told the Council that this Axon preaches anger and. . . . What is the archaic term that means the desire to do evil, because evil has been done to you?"

"Vengeance," Genaa said, and her voice was heavy with forboding. "The word was vengeance."

"Yes, that was the word Oblan used. He said that vengeance is the first goal of those who call themselves the Nekom."

"And Wassou?" Genaa asked. "Was he badly injured?"

"Yes, badly. But the healers have said that he will live. It seems he was set upon in the midheights of Skygrund. He was on his way to the new Erdling Garden,

49

where he had been working with the prospective teachers. When he was found, he was able to speak enough to say that he had been set upon by three or four men—Erdlings, although they were dressed in shubas. They rushed out at him suddenly from a thicket of end-branches and began to strike him with long sharp pieces of metal. He would surely have died except that when he fell he was near the edge of the branchpath, and he managed to push himself off and into a long free fall. His attackers followed, but his greater skill at gliding saved him. He was able to prolong his glide long after the Erdlings were forced to land on the forest floor. He was found and carried to the healers by some Erdlings from the surface city of Upper Erda. He was bloody and fainting when they reached the healers."

Again Genaa shook her head, and then sat silently for many moments, her hands pressed against her mouth. Her eyes were enormous and bleak with horror. When she spoke again her voice quivered. "Poor Wassou. He is so old and frail. Why would they wish to harm such a one?"

"Who can say?" Neric answered. "Except that he was of the Geets-kel. Perhaps the Nekom intend to take vengeance against all who were once Geets-kel."

"But why Wassou? He was the first among the Geets-kel to oppose Regle and accept our goals. And since the Rejoyning he has set an example, not only to the Geets-kel but to all who were once Ol-zhaan. He was among the first to leave his palace and take a nid-place in a guild home. And no one has done as much to hasten the preparation of the Erdling nid-places and Gardens."

"I know. It would seem that vengeance is a weapon that wounds the innocent."

"What will be done to them—the Nekom?" Genaa asked ". . . to those who attacked Wassou?"

"I'm not sure. There is to be an emergency meeting of the Council in an hour's time, to discuss what must be done."

Genaa sighed. Like Neric, she had spent the morning at a Senate meeting, except that she had met with Kindar, in Orbora. But she, too, had returned exhausted and unjoyful. Throughout the morning each person who had appeared before the Senate had been desperately troubled and fearful. Although the Kindar had been urged repeatedly to bring any problem concerning the Rejoyning to the immediate attention of the Senate, they would not do so. In the face of extreme anxiety, frustration, or even fear, they chanted hymns of Peace, practiced rituals of joyfulness, and consumed larger and larger quantities of Berry. Until at last, when the burden had grown beyond the reach of ritual or Berry, they came to the Senate desperate and demoralized.

Among the petitioners whom Genaa had seen that morning, had been a Kindar carpenter whose trencher knives and chisels had been replaced by Erdling tools— and he was certain that the tools were cursed. Their very efficiency—the sharp bite that shaped the wood with such enchanted swiftness—was proof, to him, of their accursedness. Twice already, they had caused him small injuries. They were, he was certain, only waiting for the right moment to take his life.

There had been, also, two Kindar bond-pairs whose nid-places were in the farheights, near some of the first Erdling height-dwellers. They were afraid that they were being poisoned by the smoke that came from the Erdling hearthfires, and of the effect of the rough and tempestuous Erdling children on their own children's peacefulness and Joy. They were even terrified, although they hesitated to say so, for the lives of their pets and their children at the hands of the flesh-eaters, who were now their neighbors.

But the most troubling of all, twice that morning, Kindar had been brought before the Senate who were far gone in Berry-dreaming and clearly not suffering from the effects of the Wissenberry alone. Genaa had been horrified to learn that they had eaten the fruit of the pavo-vine. Growing only in the farheights, this parasitic plant produced a small green berry that was capable of causing extreme hallucinations and was quickly and incurably addictive. Eaten regularly, it soon brought about a dream state from which there was no awakening. For generations the use of the pavo-berry had been forbidden and almost unheard of in Green-sky. But now, since the withering of the Root, the Wissenberry seeemd to be gradually losing its milder dream-inducing power, and there were those who were turning to the deadly fruit of the pavo-vine.

All morning Genaa had searched for answers to difficult questions, and when midday had arrived, bringing a free half-day, she had returned to her nid-chamber determined to spend the free hours in rest. And now, a new and even more frightening problem had arisen and, as a member of the Council, she would have to go to the emergency meeting to search for a solution. Genaa sighed again and rose wearily from her nid. She put on the shuba she had so recently removed and then stood limply, head drooping, while Neric helped her with the wing-panels, tying the fastenings tightly at wrist and ankle.

Neric regarded her anxiously. "Wouldn't you like to rest a little longer?" he asked. "There is still time before the meeting."

Genaa shook her head. "It would be useless. I couldn't rest now."

Reaching out, Neric pulled her to him caressingly, thinking to comfort her with the ritual of close communion, but she pushed him away.

"This is not the time for Love-rituals," she said. "How could we comfort each other, knowing what has happened to poor Wassou—and what has happened to the Rejoyning."

Turning away she walked to the window and stood looking out into the soft green of the forest.

"What has happened?" she asked again. "Will it fail, the Rejoyning?"

Neric went to stand beside her at the window, but he did not try to answer.

"We were all so sure," Genaa said. "So sure that when the truth was told and the Erdlings free, evil would be conquered, and all would be as it was in the early days. Were we wrong? Would it have been better to leave things as they were?"

"I don't know," Neric said. "I have wondered, too, at times."

"Raamo," Genaa said suddenly. "I can't bear to think what this will do to Raamo. He has been so troubled lately—and now this."

"Where is Raamo?" Neric asked. "At the Vine Palace again?"

"Yes. With the children. He goes there every day to see if they are well."

"I know," Neric said. "He is seldom here at the youth

54

hall. It has been several days since I have spoken with him." Neric smiled ruefully. "And there are few enough here whom I may speak to. Who would have thought that life in a youth hall could be so lonely. I wonder what they think of us, Genaa, that they leave us so much alone."

They both stood quietly a moment, trying to understand what had happened to them. In their presence the young Kindar seemed at times to be both intrigued and embarrassed, awed and suspicious, worshipful and resentful. It was obvious that in their minds Neric and Genaa were still Ol-zhaan, as well as Rejoyners and members of the Joined Council, and as such, impossible to accept into the warm and easy bonds of youth hall life. Their presence in common room or food-taking chamber invariably signaled the end of games and dances and a hushing of laughter and conversation. In all the time since their arrival in the hall, there had been only two exceptions to this rule of exclusion—and they had been exceptional indeed. The two had been the Erdlings, the first and, as yet, the only Erdlings to take up residence in a Kindar youth hall.

These Erdling hall-dwellers were Sard, at twenty-one only a little older than Neric himself, and Mawno, perhaps a year younger. Only two months before, when they had first arrived at the Stargrund Youth Hall, they had regarded the former Ol-zhaan with even more suspicion and hostility than did the Kindar. But in a remarkably short time, the attitude of the Erdlings had changed to warm and open acceptance. Neric was not sure why.

Perhaps it was in the Erdling nature, with their unpatterned and informal relationships, to be able to make such sudden and seemingly complete changes. There was also the fact that the Erdlings had found their Kindar hallmates extremely resistant to their offers of friendship. And that, too, might have encouraged the Erdlings to resort more quickly to friendship with former Ol-zhaan.

Sard and Mawno were true Erdlings, and the friendship had been enlightening, if not always comfortable. They were, Neric thought, like a pair of treebears, playful and charming and yet uncomfortably unpredictable. Sturdy and golden in appearance, boisterous and abrupt in manner, they seemed to Neric to be entirely typical products of Erdling culture. And yet they claimed to be just the opposite—daring and unconventional explorers and innovators. The very fact of their presence in the Kindar youth hall proved, they said, that they were rebels.

"My parents won't tell anyone where I'm living," Mawno said once. "They haven't even told the rest of our clan."

"Why not?" Genaa had asked.

"They say I've disgraced them."

Mawno was lying, sprawled like a sima, on the floor of Neric's chamber, his long hair and swarthy golden skin contrasting strangely with the elegance of the elaborately embroidered shuba he was wearing. He would have looked much more natural, Neric had thought, in the tight-fitting fur of his native costume.

The conversation had taken place only a few days before, on the afternoon of a full free day. Raamo had been there, briefly, and he and Genaa, along with the two Erdlings, had gathered in Neric's chamber to relax and entertain themselves as best they could. Not far away, in the large common room, there was singing and laughter, which they knew would cease abruptly if any one of them appeared.

"Disgraced?" Genaa had asked. "What have you done that is disgraceful?"

"Nothing," Mawno said smiling. "It is simply that I have chosen to live in a youth hall. My family, like most Erdlings, does not approve of allowing young people to leave their home caverns until they are old enough to choose bond-partners. And there are forbiddances against some of your rituals—except to the bonded."

Mawno had lowered his eyes as he spoke and his face flushed, as if someone had used a term of extreme unjoyfulness in a public place.

"I know," Neric had said. "Those of us who were assigned to the Erdling Senates were instructed on such matters. There are many such strange taboos and forbiddances in Erda. They became necessary, I think, because of insufficient training in Peace and Joy. When the strong emotions of communion are not properly trained and patterned, they can lead to danger—and to the necessity for strange taboos."

"I disagree." It was Sard who spoke. During most of the discussion he had been pacing around the room, but now he stopped before Neric and stared down at him. Tall and fine-boned, with a mind that cut like an Erdling knife, he could almost have passed for a Kindar, except for his lack of graces. His blunt, unmannered denial was typical, Neric thought. "Our taboos grew out of our lack of access to the ingredients necessary to the production of youth-wafers. Where food and living space is limited, as it has been in Erda, and the means to produce contraceptives is lacking, youth halls would, in-

57

deed, be dangerous. Like all taboos, ours grew out of practical necessity, and only much later began to be related to such impractical matters as good and evil. But whatever their origin, our taboos are no more strange to you than your everlasting rituals and ceremonies are to us."

Turning suddenly towards Raamo, Sard's face underwent another of its completely unpredictable changes. Smiling, he said, "Don't be concerned little Ol-zhaan. I am not unjoyful towards your comrade. It is only that I cannot resist matching my dull Erdling wits with your learned friend."

"Dull, indeed," Genaa had said laughing. "Your Erdling wits are as sharp as your Erdling steel, and I think you know it very well."

Sard looked at Genaa and there was something in his gaze that made Neric think of the red glow of Erdling hearthfire. "Well," Sard had said softly, "if my wits are like Erdling steel, yours are like a Kindar raindrop in the sunshine—clear and dazzling." He stared at Genaa for a long moment and when he spoke again the red glow was in his voice as well. "Who would have thought an Ol-zhaan could be so lovely."

The discussion had left Neric with a strange confusion of feelings, feelings that he found to be unnameable and, for the most part, not particularly joyful. Remembering only added to his present state of unjoyfulness. Dropping his head into his hands, he sat for a long time in a decidedly un-Kindarlike attitude of dejection. He did not lift his head until he felt Genaa's hand on his shoulder.

"Come," she said wearily, "we must help decide what must be done about the Nekom."

CHAPTER SIX

W hen Genaa and Neric left the youth hall, they made their way along the public branchpaths, through the heart of the city, to the great public assembly hall of Orbora. Although it had long ago been decided that the permanent quarters of the Joined Council would be in the Temple Grove in the meeting chamber of the Ol-zhaan, they had not, as yet, made the move. Nearly all of the Council members were in favor of the change. It was agreed that it was only fitting that the beautiful chamber in the Grove should be used by the Council—now the highest authority in Green-sky. However, the move to the Grove continued to be postponed, at the request of the delegates from Erda.

It was not that the Erdlings were unappreciative of the opportunity to use and enjoy the luxurious surroundings that had for so long been reserved for the exclusive use of the Ol-zhaan. It was simply a matter of convenience, the convenience of some of the Erdling Councilors whose age and physical condition made a hardship of the long climb to the heights. For some, even to reach the lowest grundlevel by means of the newly constructed hanging stairways was far from easy. And to go still higher along narrow branchways, ramps and ladders would be not only very difficult, but dangerous as well, since several of the more elderly had not yet mastered the use of the shuba, and perhaps never would.

So the emergency meeting of the Joined Council was convened in the great assembly hall. And it was there, just outside the great archway of the entrance, that Neric and Genaa came upon Raamo. Simply dressed in an unadorned shuba of pale brown, such as was often worn by apprentices and students, Raamo looked strangely out of place among the other Councilors, a child among adults, a shy, uncertain boy among men and women long accustomed to honor and responsibility. Even Genaa, who was approximately the same age, seemed older. To Neric, it seemed a matter of gifts—and time. Genaa's brilliance of mind and body was a temporal gift, and having received it so early had aged her, making her wise and beautiful beyond her years. But the gifts that had been given to Raamo were ageless—beyond the realm of days and years.

When Raamo saw Neric and Genaa, his pale face lightened briefly with a smile and he hurried to meet them. But his eyes were troubled.

"What is it?" Raamo asked. "The messenger told me only that there was to be an emergency meeting. What is it about? Wassou?"

But at that moment the huge double doors of the hall were opened, and the Councilors surged past them.

"Wassou was injured by the Nekom," Neric said briefly. "He is still alive. Come, we will hear it all soon enough."

Along with the other members of the Council, Raamo,

Neric, and Genaa made their way down the long central aisle between the rows of tendril benches, to the steps that led up to the high platform where the meeting table-board was set. The Council consisted of forty-seven members—twenty Erdlings and twenty Kindar, plus the seven who had faced D'ol Regle and brought about the Rejoyning. In spite of the short notice, nearly all were present to face what could be the greatest threat to the future of Green-sky since that first day when the power of uniforce had taken the tool-of-violence from the hands of D'ol Regle.

The meeting was long and painful. What had happened was without precedent. There were not even any publicly recognized words to discuss what had been done, since the archaic terms were known only to those who had been Ol-zhaan. And the description of the deed was agonizingly embarrassing to all the delegates, and to the Kindar in particular.

It seemed impossible to believe that such a thing had actually happened, and even more impossible to realize that it was necessary for them to discuss such an un-natural and inhuman event in a public place. And when the exact nature of the deed had been made clear to all, there followed an equally unthinkable duty. It was the responsibility of the Council to decide the fate of Axon Befal and the others who had attempted to take the life of the old man, Wassou.

Except for the banishment of the Verban, of which the Kindar had been innocent and ignorant, all offenders in Green-sky had always been ordered to appear at one of the Chambers of Justice. There they were examined and asked to justify their behavior in terms of its rela-tionship to the gifts of the Spirit—to Peace and Joy and

61

Love. If their explanation was considered to be lacking, or if the offense was repeated, they were assigned to a remedial seminar. At the nearest Garden they attended classes in Peace—or in whatever Spirit-skill seemed appropriate, in that its lack seemed to be responsible for their offense. There, among the youngest children, they relearned the rituals and ceremonies, the skills and practices, that would make their misdeeds unnecessary. In almost all cases the method was highly effective. But in this case such a remedy was obviously impossible.

Slightly more severe measures were often used in Erda, but even these were not appropriate for this. It seemed unlikely that public reprimand, heavier workload, organized ostracism or even reduced food ration would deter the Nekom from pursuing their terrible goal.

At last, after hours of debate, a verdict was reached. Axon Befal and those of his followers who had participated in the attack would be found and examined, and if they were guilty, they would be taken to the new surface city that was just being constructed below the smallest and most distant Kindar city, Farvald. Guards would be posted, and the offenders would live and work under constant surveillance for a period of at least two years. Their movements would not be hindered within the boundaries of the city, but if they left Farbelo at any time, for any reason, the Council would immediately be notified.

On leaving the assembly hall, Raamo and Neric and Genaa walked for a short way together. Raamo was silent, deep in thought, and Genaa watched him with concern. His face was as open and unblocked as that of a three-year-old, and it was not necessary to be able to

62

pense to know that he was in great mind-pain.

"Are you coming with us to the youth hall, then?" she asked when they turned off the main branchpath.

Raamo looked up suddenly, roused from his thought-taking. "No," he said, looking around in bewilderment. "I meant to go on towards the rampway. I was going back to the Vine Palace. I must see if Pomma and Teera are . . . if they are all right."

"All right?" Neric asked. "Why wouldn't they be all right?"

"They were to be taken today to the harvester's guild hall in Orchardgrund. My father arranged it. Some of the members of his guild have formed a chapter of Ny-zhaan, and they asked if the children could be present at their welcoming of the members."

"A chapter of Ny-zhaan in the harvesters' guild?" Genaa asked. "The movement must, indeed, be spreading. I thought it was popular mainly among professional thought-takers—teachers from the academies, and the few former Ol-zhaan who started it."

"I think that is true," Raamo said, "for the most part. But my father was asked to attend some of their meetings, and he has become interested. I think that he had influenced some of his fellow harvesters. But I think it is true that there are not many from the craft guilds who are members of the Ny-zhaan."

"I thought the movement might be dying out," Neric said. "At least I've heard very little about them in recent weeks."

"They are few in number, I think," Raamo said, "but very dedicated."

"Dedicated? To what? I don't think I've ever heard exactly what their beliefs and rituals are."

"They don't seem to have many rituals," Raamo said. "At least, I've not heard much said concerning them. But they have many meetings."

"What do they do at their meetings if they have no rituals?" Genaa asked.

"They talk," Raamo said. "They meet together and talk. Some of them are Erdling."

"And of what do they talk?"

"They talk of the Spirit, I think, and of the teachings of Nesh-om. And of the children. They have great Love for the children."

"But if they have such great Love for Pomma and Teera, why are you fearful? Surely no harm could come to the children at a meeting of the Ny-zhaan."

"I'm not sure where the harm might come from," Raamo said. "But I think it would be best if the children were not taken out on the public branchways."

As he spoke, Raamo had been edging back towards the rampway, his manner hurried and distracted, and now he turned suddenly, and lifted his face upward and towards the east—towards the Temple Grove. "I must go now," he said, and without even the palm-touch of the shortened form of the ceremony of parting, he hurried away.

Neric shook his head. "I'm worried about him, Genaa. He seems to be greatly changed. I can no longer pense what he is thinking."

Genaa looked at him sharply. "We have all changed," she said. "But I, too, have worried about Raamo. All this—this tension and mind-pain is harder for him than for most of us. He is too much wounded by the pain of others."

As Raamo started up the Stargrund rampway, the

twilight deepened into darkness and the first drops of the night rain began to fall. The rampway was deserted, and Raamo's pace quickened. Surely the children would have been taken home to the Vine Palace by now. He had hoped to be there when they returned. He had hoped to be there, in case. . . .

For a moment the shadows that hovered at the edge of every thought concerning Pomma and Teera, seemed to be parting, and Raamo stopped. Standing very still just where the rampway met the large central platform of the Grove, he lifted his face to the warm patter of the first rain and sent his thoughts out to search the shadows —to try to see what threat was hidden there. But as always when he faced it, the shadow faded back into the darkness, leaving only a pale flicker of warning. Raamo hurried on.

When he reached the Vine Palace, the tendril gate had already been set in place, and Raamo had to blow on the entry flute and then wait for someone to arrive to release the gates. He had not waited long before Eudic appeared, an old man who had been in the service of D'ol Falla for many years.

"Have the children returned from Orchardgrund?" Raamo asked the serving man.

"Yes, D'ol Raamo," the old man replied. "They returned some time ago. I think they are now in the hall of food-taking."

"Thank you, Eudic," Raamo said. "And Eudic—you should remember to call me Raamo—only Raamo. The Council has decreed that the title D'ol is to be given only by the Council as a special honor. No one is entitled to its use now, except D'ol Falla."

The old man nodded, making a gesture of contrition.

"I know. I know, D—Raamo," he said. "But I am an old man, and habits as old as mine are hard to break."

Raamo held out his hands for the old man's palm-touch, and then hurried on. The serving man stood looking after him until he disappeared in the dimness of the long hallway.

"Too bad, too bad," the serving man muttered, his misty hair quivering around his shaking head. "It is clear that he is true Ol-zhaan—a Spirit-guided, such as were known in the early days—meant to seek the Spirit in the Peace of the Temple."

In the hall of food-taking Raamo found Pomma and Teera seated at the table-board, just as the serving man had said. With them were their parents, Herd and Kanna Eld, and Valdo and Hearba D'ok. At the head of the table the highbacked tendril chair of D'ol Falla was empty.

"Where is D'ol Falla?" Raamo asked.

"She was very tired," Hearba said. "She has already eaten and has retired to her nid-chamber. Will you share our food-taking tonight? We did not know if you planned to eat with us or at the youth hall."

"I will share your food-taking," Raamo said.

As soon as he was seated at the table-board, Raamo gave his attention to the children. They had been chattering gaily as he entered the room, but now they were silent. His sister's blue-green eyes regarded him gravely; but when he tried to meet her gaze, she looked down quickly. Her lashes curtained her eyes and, pensing, he could feel that there were other curtains between them as well. Teera, too, would not meet his eyes but, like most Erdlings, she had not learned completely to mind-block her emotions. However, Raamo could pense no more than a vague and furtive fearfulness.

"Raamo." His father, Valdo, was speaking. "I wish you could have gone with us to the meeting of the Ny-zhaan. It went very well. There was no trouble of any kind." Valdo paused, waiting for Raamo's response. It was clear that he wanted Raamo to acknowledge that he had been right, that there had been no harm in his arranging to take the children to the meeting. "There was great happiness and excitement," he went on. "Many spoke to me of how their dedication was strengthened and heartened by the presence of the children."

Raamo smiled. He knew his father well. Valdo had been a harvester for many years, and the high regard of the fellow guild members was of great importance to him.

Hearba had been watching Raamo closely, and now she asked. "The meeting of the Council. What matters were brought before it today?"

Raamo shook his head. "I will speak of it later," he said. Turning to his sister he asked, "Pomma, did you enjoy the meeting of the Ny-zhaan?"

"Yes, Raamo," Pomma answered quickly, but her eyes were still lowered, and she spoke shyly as if to a stranger. "The people were very happy that we were there. They called out my name—and Teera's—and they threw flower petals in front of us."

Suddenly Pomma was herself again, her eyes dancing and her lips twitching into a giggle. "Look," she said, "Teera still has petals in her hair."

Raamo sighed and turned his attention to mushrooms and pan in egg sauce, which had been placed before him. Perhaps he was wrong. Perhaps the children were not in such great danger after all.

CHAPTER SEVEN

"Raamo?" Wassou said incredulously. "She is bringing Raamo? I don't think. . . . Do you think I am recovered enough to . . ."

The healer, a large cheerful woman with a gift for brisk and sensible compassion, interrupted. "Of course," she said. "You are nearly well. In a few days you will be allowed to return to your own nid-place." Approaching the chair in which Wassou was sitting, she stared down at his upturned face with frank appraisal. "You are quite all right. Quite all right," she said.

When she had gone, Wassou sat for a minute longer as if immobilized by surprise. It was true, he knew— the time was coming soon when he would have to face the outside world again. All of it, without exceptions. But it seemed, somehow, too soon.

It was not yet a full month since he had been carried, more dead than alive, into this chamber at the hall of healing. He could vaguely remember his arrival, but then nothing for many days, during which time he had been kept under constant hypnosis as a shield against the pain of his injuries. It had not been until a week ago that he had been allowed his first visitor, and it had been, of course, D'ol Falla. Since then she had returned almost daily and had sat beside him for many hours, in quiet companionship, or they spoke together of the far distant past. They had spoken of the days of their youth when, as young Ol-zhaan, they had for many years shared a close communion of deep intensity. But they had said little concerning the present and almost nothing of his wounding or of his current condition.

Almost involuntarily Wassou's hand lifted, and the tips of his fingers moved very slowly across his face. The healers had told him that he had been kept in isolation for so long in order to protect him—that he was not yet strong enough to bear the strain of social contact. But he had guessed that there was greater need to protect those who might otherwise have visited him. He had not seen his face. His request for an Erdling mirror, or even a gazing bowl, had not been granted. But he could see what the Erdling knives had done to his arms and shoulders, and the tips of his fingers had told him much, more than he wished to know. And now D'ol Falla was bringing Raamo to see him.

He loved D'ol Falla. He had always loved her. But there were times when he thought that her great wisdom was like an ancient tapestry—a thing of beauty but full of unexpected holes. Was it possible that she had not forseen the effect of this meeting on the sensitive, Spirit-haunted boy.

Rousing himself, Wassou limped hastily to the windows and drew shut the hangings, shutting out the soft green glow. Then he took a long hooded cloak from the wardrobe. Placing his chair in the darkest corner of the room, he seated himself carefully, pulling the hood forward as far as it would go around his face. He had barely finished his careful arrangements when the door hangings were thrust aside and healer entered, closely followed by D'ol Falla and behind her, the boy, Raamo.

Wassou waited while his visitors spoke at some length with the healing woman. It was obvious that she was overjoyed at the opportunity to speak with Raamo who, since the Rejoyning, had become the object of almost as much reverent adoration as the holy children. At her urgent request, Raamo sang the greeting with her, and then the parting, and both in the old unshortened version, while Wassou waited in a torment of anxious anticipation. When at last the healer departed, and the boy and D'ol Falla turned to cross the darkened chamber, pity and apprehension lay like a great weight at the pit of Wassou's stomach. Then, to his horror, as D'ol Falla finished the greeting, she bent and pressed her cheek to his, dislodging his hood so that it fell back and revealed his face to Raamo's gaze. As Raamo extended his hands for the greeting, his eyes rested on Wassou's face, and the old man waited for them to widen in horror.

"It gives me great Joy to see you again after so long a time," the boy said, and his eyes spoke of Joy and of concern, but not of distress and repulsion, as Wassou had feared they would.

"And I you," Wassou said, pressing Raamo's hands between his own and struggling to keep his voice from quavering with relief and gratitude. "Please be seated, both of you. And please, draw your chairs closer so we can talk more easily. There is fresh fruit on the table by the window. Won't you have a paam or a small pan-fruit, D'ol Falla? The paams are the kind you like, the small green ones."

70

The paams reminded D'ol Falla of how the small juicy fruit had first been developed by a gifted grunspreker when she was still a very young woman, and of how Wassou had brought her a basketful as a present on the first anniversary of their meeting. And so they spoke for some time of the past, as they had done so often in the last week. But finally the talk turned to the present, and Wassou asked for news concerning events that had taken place since he had been confined to the chambers of healing. He found that, suddenly, he was eager to hear what progress had been made while he had been recovering. He asked first about the new Garden being prepared for Erdling children.

"I have not been there myself," D'ol Falla said. "But I have received reports concerning the Garden. Classes are scheduled to begin on the first day of the fifth moon. The building is almost completed, but there have been new delays in the training of teachers and in the planning of the classes. There have been many meetings between the educators, both Erdling and Kindar, and the Erdling parents, but little has been decided. The Erdling parents do not agree among themselves on how many of the traditional Kindar classes they wish to have included in their new curriculum. Most of them want their children to receive instruction in the Spirit-skills, but not all. And many are opposed to the classes in Love and Joy. There is, I'm afraid, only one area of complete agreement, and that concerns the classes in gliding and use of the shuba. The necessity for that has been demonstrated too many times to leave room for argument."

"I know," Wassou said, "only too well. There is an Erdling child in the next nid-chamber. He had only begun to take instruction and was not yet certified, but his parents allowed him to climb to the farheights with a group of his companions. He was just below the fronds of the roof trees when he fell. There is some doubt if he will ever walk again."

"It is unfortunate that some of the Erdlings have moved into the heights before there was time to prepare for their arrival. Though their impatience is understandable, of course."

"Are the immigrants to the heights still mostly young families?" Wassou asked.

"Yes." It was Raamo who answered. "Many of the older people have found that they cannot overcome their fear of heights. So they prefer the surface cities. And there are some who prefer to go on living in Erda, just as they have always done. But wherever they go, all the immigrants want private nid-places—they do not like our youth halls and guild homes."

"Yes, there are still many problems," D'ol Falla said. "And not only concerning the Gardens and nid-places. Of late, since your illness, there has been a great deal of dissatisfaction among the distributors at the public pantries and warehouses, particularly in the hall of shubas."

"The hall of shubas?" Wassou asked. "Are there then too few shubas for the immigrants. If that is true they must, indeed, be arriving in Orbora in great numbers. There has always been a great surplus of shubas in the warehouses."

Raamo smiled. "The Erdlings have become very fond of shubas. Even those who live in Erda or in surface cities and do not glide or plan to learn have discarded their tunics for shubas. Everyone in Erda has a shuba now, or two or three. That is, everyone who has a friend or relative who has immigrated and is entitled to be served at the Orbora warehouses."

"But there is more to the problem than the Erdlings' interest in shubas," D'ol Falla said. "The trouble arises from the difference in our systems of distribution. While we have always distributed necessities according to need, and all else by honor ranking, the Erdlings are used to an exchange based on small disks of metal, which are known as tokens."

"Ah yes," Wassou said, "I have heard the term. But I never realized its significance."

"The tokens are earned by service, and they can then be exchanged for anything in any amount, as long as they last. Except for food, of course, which was carefully rationed, the Erdlings are not used to any other limits on their acquisitions. So the immigrants come to our warehouses and ask for many things; and because their needs and ranking have not been established, the distributors have been reluctant to refuse them. Even the goods that have been, by long tradition, reserved for Kindar of high honor, such as pan-wood furniture and the most richly embroidered shubas, have been asked for and given to the Erdling immigrants."

"The silkhouses have been working extra hours and on free days, but still there are not enough shubas," Raamo said. "And Kindar who must glide in ragged shubas are made unjoyful to know that fine new shubas are being worn now in the mines of Erda."

"A new calling should be made for apprentices to the silkworkers' and embroiderers' guilds," Wassou suggested.

"It has already been done, and several times. But the skills are not quickly learned," D'ol Falla said. "And the time cycle from moth to worm to woven silk cannot be hastened. It will be some time before the number of shubas produced can be greatly increased."

"Yes, yes, of course." Wassou shook his head. "Well, well. We forsaw that there would be many problems, but I think no one guessed that a shortage of shubas would be among them. But then, we predicted some that have not come to pass. One in particular. Regle has not returned to Orbora. We have been very fortunate in that respect. I would never have guessed that Regle would let seven months go by without returning to Orbora to try to vindicate himself—and to sow dissension between Erdling and Kindar. He still has not been seen?"

"No, he has not been seen, but—"

"But what?"

"Last week it was reported to the Council that a harvester who had arrived early in the orchard saw three men carrying heavy bags leaving the pan-grove. The harvester did not recognize them, but from his description it seems likely that two of the men were Tarn and Pino, two Kindar serving men who disappeared with Regle on the day of the Rejoyning."

"And the third?"

"The harvester did not see his face, but he was wearing a white shuba."

"A white shuba. An Ol-zhaan then. D'ol Regle himself?"

"No. The man was short and slighter in build. It could not have been Regle. But there are others who disappeared—other Ol-zhaan. D'ol Salaat, of course, and then soon afterwards, Ruuro and Povaal. And recently there have been a few others."

"What can it mean?"

"I don't know," D'ol Falla said. "But it is possible

74

that Regle has established a settlement somewhere in the open forest and is gathering around him all those whose opposition to the Rejoyning has caused them to flee Orbora. It is a troublesome thought."

"And Axon Befal? Has he remained in exile?"

"Yes. He and the three others who helped in the attack are still living in Farbelo, being watched by Erdling guards. They seem to be living quietly. There have been no recent reports of meetings or speeches."

As D'ol Falla spoke, she glanced anxiously at Raamo and, following her gaze, Wassou saw that Raamo had risen to his feet. His face was very pale, and his eyes were shadowed. He began to move slowly towards the doorway with a stiff, shuffling gait.

"What is it, Raamo?" D'ol Falla said sharply.

The boy started, and then smiled distractedly. "I think, perhaps I had better go now," he said. "There is to be a ceremony at the Temple—the Hymns to Nesh-om— I promised that I would take part in the singing."

"Yes," D'ol Falla said. "I, too, am going to the ceremony. But I will stay a little longer with Wassou. Go on ahead, Raamo, and I will meet you there soon."

Raamo sang the parting and was almost to the doorway when he turned back to Wassou. "I have been asked to be present at the first day of classes at the new Garden," he said. "When it is over, I will come again to tell you about it."

"I thank you, Raamo," the old man said. "I will be most anxious to hear. The Garden has been much in my thoughts these last few days."

When the boy was gone, Wassou turned to D'ol Falla, frowning. "What was it? Is the boy ill, or was it caused by something that we said? I had expected—feared—that when he saw me, he might be . . ." the old man's scarred face twisted into a rueful smile. ". . . but there was nothing—he seemed hardly to have noticed, but now this . . ."

"I think it was because we spoke of Axon Befal," D'ol Falla said. "As a member of the Council, Raamo was required to attend the judging of Axon and his followers. He sat in the great hall all day, staring at the Nekom, and then for three days he was very ill. He did not eat or speak. I think his Spirit was sickened by what he saw."

"But yet he looked at me—at my face—without fear or revulsion . . ."

Rising slowly to her feet, D'ol Falla went to Wassou and took his wounded face between her hands. "Dear friend," she said. "When Raamo looked at you, he saw a sane and healthy Spirit. It was in the Nekom that he saw mutilation."

CHAPTER EIGHT

S everal days after visiting Wassou in the chambers of healing, Raamo was at the evening food-taking at the Vine Palace. He was to go to the opening of the new Garden for Erdling children the next morning and Pomma and Teera were begging to be allowed to go with him.

"My mother said that my clan brother, Charn, will be at the new Garden," Teera said. "It has been so long since I've seen Charn. And Pomma has never seen him. I know that Pomma would like Charn. Couldn't we go with you to the new Garden?"

"Yes, Raamo. Please take us with you," Pomma begged. "We're so tired of staying in the palace all the time."

"No, Pomma," Hearba said. "It will be a celebration for the people who have worked to build the new Garden. The builders and planners and the Erdling families. I'm afraid it would only be a distraction if you and Teera were there."

Pomma stared at her mother, her chin held high. "They would want us to come," she said. "I know they would want us to come. They would be *honored*."

For a moment Hearba returned her daughter's stare. "Pomma," she said through tight lips, and then for a time she said nothing more. At last she sighed and saying, "I am going to my chamber to chant a Hymn of Peace," she turned and went away.

Watching, Raamo was aware, once more, of the faint and shadowy warning he had so often felt in the months since the Rejoyning. Going to his sister he held out both hands for her palm touch. "Pomma," he said, "I want to speak with you. It has been a long time since we spoke deeply."

But Pomma quickly put her hands behind her and backed away. "Not now," she said. "Please not now, Raamo. I—I am very tired. I think I'll just go to my chamber now to rest. Are you coming, Teera?"

Pomma left the hall hastily, but Teera lingered for a moment.

"Will you look for Charn?" she asked. "Will you speak to him and give him my greetings?"

"I will. And I will invite him to come here to the palace to see you and Pomma. Perhaps he might be able to come quite often. I know it has been hard for you and Pomma to live as you have in the past months— shut away here in the palace."

Teera threw her arms around Raamo delightedly, and then ran after Pomma, leaving Raamo to think, as he had so many times before, about his worries for the children.

They had changed since the Rejoyning, of that there could be no doubt. Yet nothing really fearful had happened. It was not a tragedy, after all, if children of nine years were sometimes petulant and demanding or even secretive and troubled. But when Raamo closed his eyes and imaged the faces of Pomma and Teera, a cloud still hovered, as threatening as before.

Early the next morning Raamo left the Temple Grove by way of the great archway and Stargrund ramp, but as he reached Startrunk, instead of continuing downward, he began to climb higher. He had intended to glide directly down to the broad public branchways and then make his way on foot to Skygrund and the new Garden, but suddenly he had an urgent yearning for the bright clarity of the farheights. He would have time to remain for a short while in the heights and then, by starting his glide from far up among the rooftree fronds, he might be able to reach Skygrund, far to the west, in one long glide.

As he climbed, he began to feel a lightening of the burdens that had so often oppressed him since the Rejoyning. Where they came from he did not know. Not from any certain knowledge. There were many among the Rejoyners who were better informed than he, and they seemed still to be hopeful, in spite of the many problems that had arisen.

Nor did his anxiety come from any foreknowledge. He had had no foretelling visions concerning the future of the Rejoyning, except for the warning that seemed to relate in some vague way to Pomma and Teera. Yet his heavy weight of unjoyfulness had seemed to grow with the days and weeks—as fears and misunderstandings spread and grew between the Kindar and the Erdlings— until it seemed now to him that fear and mind-pain rode on the air in Orbora. But in the cool bright air of the farheights, the burden was gone, as if it had been left behind, far below on the crowded branchways of the city.

Raamo stayed as long as he could among the roof-fronds, moving slowly westward, stopping to rest now and then in a rocking nid of leaf and twig. But time was passing, and he was expected at the Garden, so at last he began to look downwards for a clear glidepath leading toward Skygrund. Soon, coming to an endbranch free of Vine and leaf, he saw below him a long narrow twisting flightpath; and leaping out, he launched himself into open space.

For the first few moments he fell free to gain impetus, his arms held close to his sides. Then, with a skill born of long experience, he spread his wing-panels and swooped upwards. Still gliding swiftly from the force of his first fall, he banked around a stand of Vine, dropped to avoid a grundbranch, and entered a wide glidepath leading toward the west. Within a few minutes he was landing on the wide branchway on the lowest level of Skygrund, only a short distance from the entry-platform of the new Garden.

Joining a stream of late arriving Erdlings, both children and adults, Raamo made his way into the building —a cluster of hanging and cantilvered classrooms arranged around a central platform. A small temporary stage had been erected in the middle of the central platform, and it was around this stage that the crowd had begun to gather. As he entered the platform, Raamo began to be recognized, and soon the Erdling families were pressing around him, jostling and shoving good-naturedly as they struggled to get a glimpse of the young Rejoyner. In their open Erdling faces Raamo saw curiosity and friendly interest, and here and there a bit of suspicious doubtfulness. But he pensed no real ill will; and to those who were nearest, he reached out in mind-touch, and with the natural Erdling ability to pense emotions, they reacted quickly and warmly.

The ceremony was short and simple, and afterwards Raamo spoke briefly to some of the Erdling teachers and to D'ol Birta. Birta, as she was now called, had once been in charge of all the Gardens; and, since the Rejoyning, she had taken a special interest in helping to establish the new centers of learning for the children of the Erdling immigrants. From Birta and the others, Raamo learned much that he could tell Wassou on his next visit. When it was almost time for him to leave, Raamo spoke to the chief-teacher about Teera's clan brother, Charn Arnd.

"Charn Arnd," the teacher said. "I am not yet familiar with the names of all our children. But I shall inquire, and if he is here, I will send him to speak with you."

Raamo was waiting in a small ante-chamber when the boy approached. He entered hesitantly, a sturdy, tawny-skinned Erdling child, his gray eyes wide with amazement at so strange a summons. Standing before Raamo, he stared at him curiously for several moments before he spoke.

"Hello," he said at last. "My name is Charn. Did you want to see me?"

"Greetings, Charn," Raamo said, extending his hands. "I am Raamo."

"Yes, I know," Charn said. "Everyone knows who you are. You are a Rejoyner and the brother of the holy child, Pomma."

"I am Pomma's brother," Raamo agreed. "And I am also a friend of Teera Eld. And you are Teera's clan-brother, are you not."

81

Charn grinned delightedly. "Yes," he said. "I am Teera's clan-brother." But then his smile faded. "That is, I was, when we all lived in Erda. But there are no clans in Orbora. I don't even know if Teera remembers me any more, now that she is holy and famous."

"She remembers you very well—and she has asked me to speak to you and invite you to visit her at the Vine Palace in the Temple Grove."

"At the Vine Palace?" Charn stared at Raamo in amazement. "But how do I get there? And how do I get them to let me in?"

"I will tell you how to get there. And the people who tend the palace gates will know that you are to be admitted."

Charn's smile returned and grew broader. "All right," he said. "Tell Teera I will come. I'll come on the next free day."

"That will be fine. Teera will be very happy when I tell her that you are coming."

Charn's forehead wrinkled suddenly. "I'm not sure that I'll know how to . . . how to speak to her anymore. I'm not sure . . ." Pausing, he dropped his eyes, his face reddening, ". . . I'm not sure if I know how to talk to a holy person."

Raamo smiled. "I think you should speak to her just as you always have. I think you will find it very easy."

Charn shook his head thoughtfully, but then suddenly he smiled. "Yes," he said. "That must be true. Because people say that you are also holy, and you are very easy to speak to."

This time it was Raamo's face that flushed, and for a moment he could think of nothing more to say. But the boy was staring at him eagerly and after a time he thought to ask Charn about the new Garden.

"I don't like it," Charn said with Erdling bluntness. "I didn't want to come here."

"What is it that displeases you about the new Garden?" Raamo asked.

"It's not that," Charn said. "It's just that I liked the old one better. The one the Kindar go to. I liked it very much, even though there weren't many Erdlings there— only me and my brothers and a few others."

"Why were there so few?" Raamo asked.

"I don't know." Charn shrugged impatiently. "Because of parents. Some of the Erdling parents don't like all of the classes that are taught there. And the Kindar ones think we are too rough and noisy, and that we might teach their children to hurt each other and to eat lapans. But my parents say that we are all Kindar now together, and we should go to the Garden together. And I liked it there. I have lots of friends at the old Garden, and now I won't get to see them very much."

Charn's face darkened as he spoke, but the cloud passed quickly. "Tell Teera, greetings," he said. "Tell her I'll see her on the next free day."

As Raamo was leaving the Garden, he once more saw the woman who was now called Birta. She was standing near the entryway speaking to one of the teachers, and when she saw Raamo, she called to him.

"Raamo," she said, "if you are going back to the city center by branchway, I will walk with you."

"I thank you," Raamo said, "but I am late, and I can reach the Grove faster by gliding. Do you wish to glide with me?"

"No. I must go first to the center today by way of Silkgrund and the public pantries. But there is a glidepath nearby that you may want to take. When you reach the midheights, take the second northeast branch. It would seem to be leading in the wrong direction, but it bends back and touches on a good glidepath towards the Grove."

"Thanking Birta, Raamo began his climb to the midheights of Skygrund. He climbed hurriedly at first, but there was much to think about, and by the time he reached the first midlevel branches, his pace had slackened. When he reached the second northeast branch, he was walking slowly, deep in thought. Suddenly, almost in mid-step, he stopped and listened. There was only silence, a deep, unnatural, birdless hush. He realized then, that what had stopped him had not been a true sound, but something deeper and more inward.

It was not a sending. It did not flow freely. It reached him fitfully—thin and wispy—like the oozing breath of poisonous gases. Like the intermittent escape of thoughts too violent to be contained by even the most feverish blocking.

A few feet beyond where he stood on the narrow branchpath, a cluster of endbranches intersected a tangle of Vine, forming a dense leafy thicket. As Raamo stood transfixed and staring, one leaf quivered and then another. A curtain of Vine parted, and for a fraction of a second something gleamed like a ray of sunlight reflected in peering eyes.

Then it came again—the poisonous whisper of thought—and stepping suddenly backward into empty space, Raamo let himself fall. He dropped down and down for a great distance before he leveled into a glide that carried him towards the city center and the great public branchways of Broad and Stargrund. Landing

84

near a large group of people who were gathered around the newsinger's platform near Broadtrunk, he mingled with the crowd. He waited there, among the closely packed bodies, until the fear had faded, and then, by way of the heavily traveled ladders of Startrunk, he made his way back to the Temple Grove.

That night Raamo's dreams were full of dark thickets that bulged and quivered with monstrous anticipations, and in the morning he went to the nid-place of the Chief Mediator to speak with him privately.

Afterwards he was somewhat comforted. In the telling of what had happened—or seemed about to happen— he realized that he was not certain. That his fear had come from a fleeting feeling rather than anything actually seen or heard. And Hiro had agreed that he might well have been mistaken.

So in the days that followed he tried to forget the dark quivering thicket and remember only the good the day at the Garden had brought: Wassou's pleasure when he heard about the Garden, and Teera's Joy in her reunion with her clan-brother. It was good to see the three children playing together. Watching them racing through the corridors of the palace or huddled together whispering mysteriously, Raamo's fear for his sister and Teera seemed to diminish. Their games with Charn were rowdy and careless, childishly unconcerned with great honors and responsibilities, and in some undefined way the children seemed less threatened.

CHAPTER NINE

I t was late at night, and the evening rains had long since begun to fall, when a short, stocky figure, dressed in a long hooded cape, entered a muddy sidepath in the surface city of Upper Erda. The constant trampling of many feet had destroyed the spongy moss and topsoil of the forest, and the path had become a morass of ankle-deep mud. But the man who walked alone on East Pathway Three seemed not to notice the thick ooze that was coating his feet and the skirt of his flowing robe of lapan hide. His attention was, obviously, on more urgent matters. As he walked, his head turned rapidly from side to side, and he paused to stare cautiously down every crosspath.

When at last he stopped, it was before a long, low building fashioned of rough-hewn logs and roofed with a poorly woven thatch of frond. Going first to a low window, he squatted down and peered inside. For some time he continued his scrutiny, changing his position twice in order to inspect every corner of the interior. He stood, then, and going to the entryway, he pushed aside the doorhanging of soggy lapan hide and stepped inside.

The building he had entered was a lapan-house, one

of several that had sprung up in recent months in Upper Erda. Specializing in cooking and serving the flesh of lapan and plak hen, the lapan-houses were patronized by immigrant Erdlings who had moved into the Kindar city of Orbora, but who had not yet become Kindar in their tastes and appetites. Only a few among them had renounced the eating of flesh. There were, in fact, some who daily defied the Council's request that they refrain from cooking or eating flesh in their nid-places and continued to terrify their Kindar neighbors with their smoking hearth-fires and the smells of burning flesh. But the largest number, while honoring the Council's ruling, returned often to the surface cities and the newly established lapan-houses to satisfy their taste for fried lapan or roasted plak hen.

Since there had been no public eating houses in Erda, no tradition dictated the cost of a hot meal; but the Erdling hearth-keepers were enterprising and inventive, and the charges tended to be flexible and open to negotiation. A plate full of hot mashed tarbo root and roasted lapan, washed down by a mug of pan-mead, might go for as little as five Erdling tokens or in exchange for a few paraso eggs or a basket of tree mushrooms. But now and then a hearth-keeper might ask for something as valuable as a new shuba, fresh from the looms of the Kindar silkhouses.

Due to the lateness of the hour, the lapan-house that the robed and hooded figure entered was nearly empty. Its regular patrons had long since returned to their nid-places in the heights. Most of the table-boards were empty, except for a litter of dirty plates and utensils. The light that came from two small wall lamps and the glowing coals of the hearth-fire at the far end of the room was dim, and the air was heavy with smoke and grease. Here and there rain dripped through the makeshift roof and fell into small muddy puddles on the earthen floor. In the far corner near the hearth, two men, sitting crouched over a table, looked up quickly as the newcomer entered. Leaving a dripping trail of rainwater in his wake, the figure approached the table, and a voice emerged from the shadows of the deep hood.

"Who is hearth-keeping?" the voice asked.

"Only Dergg," one of the men at the table answered. "The other has gone home. It is safe."

Taking off his soaked and dripping cape and throwing it across a nearby chair, the newcomer sat down at the table. He was dressed in a shuba, its softly shimmering folds contrasting strangely with his thick, graceless body, as well as with the long and heavy metal instrument that hung on a leather band at his waist.

"Dergg," he called. "Dergg. Come out here."

A minute or two passed before a touseled-haired, sleepy-eyed youth appeared in a small doorway near the hearth. He was dressed in Erdling fashion in a fur tunic, except that his long apron, stained and grease-spotted, had been fashioned of torn shuba silk. His wide flat face was sullen with sleepy resentment, until sudden recognition made him start as if he had been jabbed by a roasting fork, and he scurried forward.

"Axon Befal," he stammered. "Yes, yes, Axon Befal. What can I do for you, Great Leader?"

"We are holding a meeting here," Axon said. "And we are hungry. We will have fried lapan. There will be—" He paused and looked at his two companions. "How many are coming?"

"Five, at least. Perhaps seven."

"Enough lapan for eight. And hurry."

88

The hearth-keeper burst into a flurry of activity. Scattering fresh coal on the hearth, he fanned it feverishly for several minutes and then disappeared into the back room at a trot. A moment later he returned carrying a platter of raw lapan. Within a few minutes a fresh cloud of greasy smoke billowed out from the hearth and the sound of sizzling fat filled the air.

The other Nekom arrived one by one, two more men and two women. They, like the earlier arrivals, were wearing shubas and carried, strapped to their bodies, long, sharp tools-of-violence, like the one worn by Axon Befal.

Except for muttered words of greeting, little was said until the lapan was served and eaten. At last, pushing back his empty plate, Axon leaned forward and began to speak. His voice was harsh and urgent, but low in volume, and its furtive, rasping tone blended with the rustle of raindrops in the rooffronds. In order to hear, his listeners were forced to lean far forward until their heads were almost touching over the table. Watching them, Dergg, a novice Nekom, was reminded of a huddle of scavenger beetles gathered around a tasty morsel of refuse on the forest floor.

It was clear to the hearth-keeper that, as a new recruit, he was not going to be asked to take part in the conference. But it was not clear to him whether or not he would be allowed to listen. Fearing that he would not if the matter were drawn to the attention of the members of the huddled conference, he crept as close as he dared and crouched down on the muddy floor.

He did not hear all that was said, but what he did hear filled him with a strange mixture of emotions—a bewildering blend of feverish exhilaration, fierce pride and anxious confusion.

Dergg Ursh had not been a Nekom for long, and the

belonging was still new and exciting. As a child in Erda, he had several times heard the Nekom leader speak, and he had always been excited and intrigued by the loud and stirring words. But not until he came to Upper Erda had he begun to listen in earnest. When, alone and lonely in the new surface city, he had been approached by the Nekom recruiters, he had been flattered and greatly impressed. And he had begun to listen very carefully to all the things that they told him.

It had all begun to seem very right. It was true that the Ol-zhaan, particularly those who had once been Geets-kel, had cruelly and unjustly kept the Erdlings imprisoned below the Root. And it did seem only fair that someone should be punished for so great an offense— that someone else should be forced to suffer as the Erdling had suffered for so many generations. It also seemed unfair, as Dergg had heard Axon Befal himself say, that the new Erdling immigrants were being assigned to the smallest and most simply built nid-places in the mid- and farheights of the city, rather than to the large and beautiful nid-places of the lower levels. And it seemed quite likely that, as Axon claimed, the Rejoyning had become no more than another plot against the Erdlings, and that their Councilors, Kir Oblan and the others, had allowed themselves to be duped and deceived by the Kindar Councilors, who were secretly still under the control of the Ol-zhaan. But, in the future, things would be very different.

The future, as Axon Befal described it, seemed to Dergg Ursh to be full of excitement, adventure, and glory. Axon Befal would overcome the Joined Council with its cringing Erdling and treacherous Kindar leaders, and he and his closest followers would move into the

great palaces and temples of the beautiful Temple Grove. From there, they would direct the destiny of all Green-sky, righting old wrongs and leading all who would follow, Erdling and Kindar alike, into a beautiful new era of happiness and plenty. And all those who had been loyal to Axon in these early days of trial and danger would be rewarded with privilege and honor and would be loved and respected by all the people.

Of course, it would take some time for these great changes to be brought about, and in the meantime there was much to do. In a secret hiding place in the open forest, Axon was gathering and training a large group of new recruits. It was necessary for all Nekom to learn how to climb and glide as well or better than any Kindar, and to make use of the long, sharp instrument that was called a wand-of-Befal. The wand-of-Befal would, Axon said, eventually be carried by every Erdling fortunate enough to be accepted into the society of the Nekom. Dergg looked forward eagerly to the time when he, too, would wear a wand-of-Befal and march proudly with the other Nekom up and down the great branchways of Orbora, before all the cheering people. But for the moment Dergg was a secret Nekom, and as such he was not allowed to wear a wand.

A secret Nekom was, however, a person of great importance. There were, Dergg had been told, many others besides himself. Scattered throughout the surface cities, back in Erda, and even among the immigrants in the heights, they were all engaged in carrying out duties that were absolutely essential to the glorious future of the new Green-sky.

There were secret members among the craftsmen who still worked in the caves of Erda, whose duty it was to fashion the wands-of-Befal from Erdling steel. There were others who lived with their families in Orbora and were thus able to acquire shubas for all the members. And there were many who, in various ways, contributed to the support of the forest community of full-time Nekom. Some allowed their nid-places to be used as occasional hiding places; others helped to obtain and transport food; and yet others worked as recruiters in their own neighborhoods and places of service. Dergg's assignment up to the present time had been to make food and shelter available to occasional groups of Nekom during the hours of rain and darkness. This he had been able to accomplish easily, simply by staying on as watchman after the old man who owned the lapan-house had gone home to his nid-place. So Dergg had been able to be of service to his fellow Nekom while he was, at the same time, earning the extra tokens that the old man was glad to pay to have his lapan-house guarded during the hours of darkness.

Dergg felt that he was fortunate indeed, and particularly fortunate tonight, when the Great Leader, himself, honored the lapan-house with his presence. Leaning far to one side, straining until his ears ached from the effort, Dergg tried desperately to hear and understand every syllable of the message that Axon Befal was imparting to his followers. His words were certain to be of great importance, full of wisdom and power.

But Axon Befal was still speaking too softly for Dergg to make out exactly what he was saying. His tone, however, was abrupt and full of tension, and he seemed to be reprimanding one of the Nekom officers who sat with him at the table. Dergg shivered, glad that the Great Leader's harshness was not directed at him-

93

self. But now, occasional words and phrases became clear, and it seemed that Axon was scolding one whose task it was to train the Nekom in the skill of gliding. Suddenly, Axon Befal's voice rose, almost to a mighty roar.

"Twice now we have failed," he was saying. "And each time we have failed because the Kindar were more agile and possessed greater skill at gliding. First we allowed the old man to escape from beneath the very edges of our wands, and now we have allowed one of the most dangerous and powerful of all the Ol-zhaan to elude us.

Then one of the others spoke. "Your pardon, Great Leader, but I don't understand why—"

But at that point the speaker turned his head and his voice fell, so that the rest of what he said was swallowed in the rustle of the rain on the rooffronds.

But Axon's voice was still lifted, and Dergg clearly heard his reply. "You are right in part," he said. "It is true that his name is not on our list—not yet. And we were not expecting him. Our watcher told us that the woman Geets-kel known as Birta often used the branch-path we were guarding. It was she whom we were awaiting. But he would have been an even greater prize. Is he not a member of the corrupt Council? And during the hearing against us, he hardened the hearts of the Councilors against our cause. True, he said but little, but that one does not need to speak to influence the people. Don't you remember, Harff, how he stared at us? He has great power over the people, both Erdling and Kindar. And do you imagine that, once we have come to power, he would not try to turn the people against us? No, it would have been no mistake if we had taken Raamo."

At that moment Dergg Ursh lost his balance and sat

94

down suddenly on the muddy floor of the lapan-house. Glancing his way, Axon Befal frowned and gestured for him to approach.

"Get us some more pan-mead, boy," he said. "We are thirsty."

In the supply room, behind the hearth, Dergg Ursh filled his pitcher from the barrel of musty mead and started to leave the room, but suddenly he stopped and leaned against the wall. His hands were shaking, and his head felt large and painful with confusion.

Had the leader really meant that there had been an attack on Raamo? It seemed impossible. Dergg had taken a special interest in the young Councilor since the first days of the Rejoyning. For one thing, they were almost the same age. And then, in the third or fourth month of the Rejoyning, he had actually seen Raamo, when a group of Councilors had come to speak to the people of Upper Erda. Struggling through the crowd, Dergg had found himself suddenly face to face with Raamo; and as he looked into the clear, deep eyes of the young Rejoyner, he had been stirred and shaken by a strong feeling. He did not know what the feeling meant, but it had been strong and warm and unforgettable. Surely, Axon Befal had not meant what he had seemed to be saying. Surely he had only misunderstood.

Taking a deep breath, Dergg shook his head hard to clear it of the dark confusion, which had, for a moment, almost overwhelmed him, and hurried back into the main chamber of the lapan-house.

As he poured the mead, he listened carefully, but they were no longer speaking of Raamo. Instead, Axon Befal was telling his officers of a great new plan that he had recently conceived, a plan that would greatly hasten the day when the Nekom would be welcomed into Or-bora and honored by all the people of Green-sky.

Dergg would have liked to hear more about the new plan, but this time, when he squatted down to listen, Axon Befal glanced up and ordered him from the room.

CHAPTER TEN

T he day was almost over. It was a day of full service in the month of two moons, almost ten months after the beginning of the time of the Rejoyning. In the great orchard of Orbora the harvesters were leaving the trees, laden with full packs of produce—heavy, hard-shelled braazer nuts, fruits of many varieties, and the great full-bodied panfruit so indispensable to every Kindar food-taking.

At the sound of the foreman's signal flute, many of the harvesters began the upward climb to the connecting ramps and branchways that led back to the storage halls and robing rooms of Orchardgrund, just as generations of harvesters had done before them. But now, there was also another route and another destination.

Now, at the sound of the flute, a goodly number of the heavily laden workers started to make their way downward by means of newly constructed hanging stairways that led down to the earth below. Too weighed down by their heavy packs to attempt to glide, they climbed slowly and carefully until they reached the orchard floor. Once there, they joined a procession of their fellow workers that wound its way to a number of long, low storage halls near the edge of the grund forest. There they deposited the produce that would be picked up later by Erdling carriers and transported to one of the surface cities or, perhaps, down to the caverns of Erda. These harvesters, whose job it was to supply the Erdlings who had not yet immigrated to the heights, were nearly all very young. The reason for this lay in the persistence of old fears. Veteran harvesters were not really frightened. They knew now that the terrible stories of the Pash-shan had not been true. Yet even to look at the forest floor still caused them a deep, unreasoned discomfort. So they were allowed to continue in the old ways, while the younger harvesters supplied the new Erdling storage halls.

On this particular day, as the harvesters moved out of the orchards, they were being watched by a small group hidden among the leaf-grown endbranches of a large forest grund. When the great orchard was finally deserted, the band of watchers moved out onto an open branchway. They were five in number, and one of them was wearing a shuba which, although frayed and soiled, had obviously once been white. Ten months after the abolishment of every distinction that had set the Ol-zhaan apart from their fellow Kindar, the young man who was leading the furtive advance out into the open orchard was dressed in the white shuba and the green-gold seal of the Ol-zhaan.

"All right," he said suddenly, turning back to his followers. "Quickly now. Little enough time remains before the rains. Tarn, you and Pino take the pan grove. You, Wuul, try the nut trees, and Corro, see what has been left in the fruit rows. But be sure to leave the orchard at the first drops of rain and return to the outpost. I will meet you there, and we will wait until daybreak to return to Wissen-wald."

Stepping to the edge of the high grundbranch, the Kindar workers launched themselves into space, their empty packs flapping behind them. For a moment, the young Ol-zhaan stood watching, and then moving purposefully and hastily, he began to make his way around the orchard in the direction of Orbora. The forest was dense here, with leafy endbranch thickets and heavy curtains of Vine making gliding impossible. So the traveler made his way on foot, trotting down narrow branches and scrambling through dense thickets of endgrowth. When he reached the outskirts of the city, he began to move slowly and carefully. At last he stopped and, looking carefully all around, pushed his way into a large thicket that concealed a tiny, crudely built chamber constructed of frond and woven tendril.

Except for a sagging overgrown nid, a lopsided tendril table, and a short-legged bench, the chamber was empty. It was obviously the work of children, built long ago as a secret meeting place and, apparently, now forgotten and deserted. It was, however, isolated and well hidden, qualities that made it well suited to the purposes of the young man. Seating himself on the bench, the youth settled himself to wait and rest— but he did not relax his guard or allow his vigilance to diminish. He was, after all, D'ol Salaat, holy Ol-zhaan and loyal disciple of the great D'ol Regle, on a mission of great peril and awesome responsibility.

D'ol Salaat was now an outcast, living in exile in the secret community of Wissen-wald, a day's journey to the northeast of Orbora. It was not an easy life nor, at the moment, a richly rewarding one, in terms of honor and glory. But he had faith in the inspired teachings of the glorious D'ol Wissen, in the time-tested traditions and institutions, and, most of all, in the strength and wisdom of the noble D'ol Regle.

Thus musing, D'ol Salaat had, perhaps, allowed his vigilance to relax for the merest fraction of a second, because he was suddenly aware that two persons had entered the tiny chamber and were now standing directly before him. Springing to his feet in some confusion, D'ol Salaat immediately composed himself and demanded that the newcomers recite the password and oath of allegiance to the Great Perpetuator, D'ol Regle —an oath composed some weeks before by D'ol Salaat himself. The newcomers were well known to him, Kindar who had for some time been in the service of the exiles. However, the oath and the password were a part of the new ritual for loyal Kindar and were therefore not to be neglected. When the rituals were properly completed, D'ol Salaat wasted no time in getting to the matter at hand.

"Greetings, loyal Kindar," he said, taking care to smile with gracious benevolence that the humble Kindar might not be overwhelmed at his presence. "What news do you bring me concerning the missions that you have been given to perform? You, Quon, what luck have you had in recruiting Kindar workmen?"

Quon, a pale-eyed old man with a small nervous mouth, stared at D'ol Salaat as if in consternation for some moments before he spoke. At last he stammered, "No—not—I'm afraid . . . not a great deal, Honored One. I have found four, perhaps five, who would be willing to join the community, I am sure. They speak openly of their unjoyfulness at having to live and work

100

with Erdlings and their fear for the future of Orbora under the Rejoyners. But they are older men and for the most part unskilled in the use of the metal tools of the Erdlings. Is it absolutely necessary that the recruits be those who are assigned to the use of the fire-cursed instruments of the Erdlings?"

D'ol Salaat sighed loudly, but with great patience. "I have explained the need to you before," he said. "It will be necessary for the community to establish its own orchards as quickly as possible, so that we may have an independent food supply. And in order to do so, we must quickly clear away the forest so that produce trees can be planted. For this we must have metal tools, and workmen who can use them."

The old man nodded, but weakly and without conviction. "But would it not be better for the Ol-zhaan to clear the forest by means of grunspreking, as was done when the great orchards of Orbora were planted in the early days? Cannot the Ol-zhaan deaden the grunds and rooftrees by means of grunspreking—as was done by the blessed D'ol Wissen?"

D'ol Salaat sighed again and more loudly. "Of course, the Ol-zhaan can still clear the trees by means of grunspreking. But—you see—we do not have time to wait for the trees to disintegrate after they have been deadened through grunspreking. Therefore we must make use of the Erdling tools. Certainly some of the Kindar workers must be adept in their use by now."

"Oh yes, Honored One. Some of the workmen in my own guild use Erdling tools daily now—with no fear at all. But they are, for the most part, in sympathy with the Rejoyners. I have heard some of them speak . . ." The old man paused, and his eyes fell in embarrassed confusion.

101

"Yes, yes," D'ol Salaat urged. "You have heard them speak of what?"

With his eyes still averted and his voice trembling, Quon continued, "I have heard them speak with great harshness concerning D'ol Regle. They feel great unjoyfulness towards D'ol Regle concerning the tool-of-violence and the holy . . . the two children. I think it would not be wise to speak to them of Wissen-wald and of D'ol Regle."

"Yes, I see. You are probably right. You must use your own judgment in these matters, since it would be unsafe for me to be seen in Orbora. Otherwise I would come with you to the guild halls to speak with the workers and make them see that their only hope lies with us and with D'ol Regle. So it is up to you, Quon, to make them see the truth. It is a great responsibility, and someday when D'ol Regle has returned to Temple Grove, you will be richly rewarded. And now, you, Maala. What luck have you had with your task?"

The other Kindar, a woman of middle age with a thin, firm-chinned face, stepped forward briskly. "I, too, have little to report," she said. "It is two months now since I began searching, and I have been over every inch of the palace. I have listened carefully to every conversation that I have been able to overhear; but I have, as yet, no clue to the hiding place of the tool-of-violence. Isn't it possible that it has been dismantled, broken into little pieces and the parts scattered?"

"No," D'ol Salaat said. "I have spoken to D'ol Regle concerning the matter, and he has assured me that it would be impossible. D'ol Regle told me that the tool-of-violence was constructed around a force capsule in such a way that it could not be disassembled or deactivated without releasing its power in a great consuming wave of energy that would destroy everything for miles around. He says that D'ol Falla knows this, and that she would not allow the weapon to be tampered with in any way. D'ol Regle has told me that if you have heard no one speaking of the tool-of-violence, it must mean that no one knows of its continued existence except D'ol Falla— and it must, therefore, be hidden in a place that would be accessible to her. Since she is old and fragile, it is apt to be in or near her own quarters in the Vine Palace."

"Yes, Honored One," Maala said. "I will try to search again in such places."

D'ol Salaat was disappointed. He had traveled the long distance to this rendezvous with great effort and personal risk and to what purpose? Neither of his Kindar agents had made any progress in the tasks to which they had been assigned. Their lack of success was due, he felt certain, to the fact that, like most Kindar, they were simply unable to function in a capacity that required initiative and imagination. Stifling his impatience as best he could, he asked them a last question. "Is there anything else you have learned—of which D'ol Regle should be informed? Anything which might affect the well-being of the community, and the furtherance of our holy purpose?"

The old man Quon's feet shuffled nervously and his mouth opened and closed several times in rapid succession. Obviously he was considering some form of communication.

"Yes, yes," D'ol Salaat urged with some forcefulness.

"It is about the Erdling who is called Axon Befal, Honored One. About Axon Befal and those who are his followers and are called the Nekom."

103

"Yes, yes—well?"

"There are whispers. . . . Some people are saying—that they, too, have made a community in the open forest. And that they have sharp-edged tools-of-violence. They have already made an attack upon the old man who is called Wassou, and who was once a Geets-kel—as I told you before Honored One. And after that they were exiled to Farbelo. But now there are rumors that they have left Farbelo and have built a community in the forest."

"The old man is *D'ol* Wassou," D'ol Salaat corrected. "An Ol-zhaan is always an Ol-zhaan. Does he still live?"

"Yes, Honored One. D'ol Wassou was badly harmed, but he still lives. There are whispers, however, that the Nekom are planning to harm others—perhaps many others."

A thrill of fear raced upward from the soles of D'ol Salaat's feet to the top of his head. "It this true? Is there any proof?" Turning to the woman he asked, "Have you heard of this, also?"

"No," she said. "I have heard nothing recently that concerned the Nekom."

"It is not yet widely known," Quon said. "There has been no mention of it in the announcements of the Joined Council. It has only been whispered of among the Kindar who work daily with Erdling craftsmen."

"I see," D'ol Salaat said, struggling to keep his voice firm and steady. "It is probably no more than baseless rumor. But I will speak of it to D'ol Regle when I return to Wissen-wald."

Since the Kindar seemed to have nothing further to report, D'ol Salaat dismissed them; but as they were leaving, walking backward with their arms outstretched in the ritual gesture of reverence and respect, as was proper for Kindar leaving the presence of an Ol-zhaan, a further thought occurred to D'ol Salaat. Calling the woman back, he gave her a final exhortation.

"Maala," he said. "The rumor of which Quon spoke is undoubtedly false. But if it should not be—if there is a possibility that the Nekom are preparing for violence— it is even more urgent that you successfully complete the assignment that has been given to you. It is absolutely imperative that you find the ancient tool-of-violence and deliver it to D'ol Regle in Wissen-wald."

As he spoke, he stared sternly at the Kindar woman, and she trembled before his gaze.

"Yes, Honored One," she said. "I will search for it night and day."

iro D'anhk found himself fervently muttering the words of the Hymn of Peace—precisely as would any well-trained Garden child when faced with a situation that might cause unjoyfulness. Pushing aside the tapestries, he stepped out onto the balcony of his nid-chamber. At first he saw nothing to indicate the source of the disturbance. The broad branchpath below his balcony was deserted; but the shrieks and shouts continued, and their source was clearly not far away.

Then, as he watched, a thicket of leafy endbranches quivered violently and erupted two children who, scrambling to their feet, began to race in circles, screaming in obviously joyful abandon. Unseen on his balcony, Hiro examined with curiosity both the screaming children and his own reaction.

The children were, perhaps, four or five years old, and although they were both dressed as Kindar in silken shubas, the tawny skin and stocky build of one revealed his Erdling parentage. Undoubtedly the child of one of the young Erdling families who had recently immigrated into the farheights of the city. The other, lightboned and agile as a sima, his small head covered by a close-cropped mass of bright curls, was clearly Kindar. Watching their play, a senseless and almost hysterical game of chase and be chased, aroused in Hiro a strange feeling of anxiety. The anxiety, he realized, had several causes and arose from many levels.

On the immediate level, it was simply very troubling, when there was so much to be accomplished, to have his thinking disturbed by unnecessary noise. It was only a month until the Celebration, decreed by the Joined Council, to commemmorate the first anniversary of the Rejoyning. It was necessary for him to think clearly and without distraction. Each day, it seemed, there was less to celebrate, and yet the long-awaited ceremony must take place. Yet what should it be? What could it be?

On another level, his uneasiness at the sound of the children was unreasoned, almost instinctive, and arose from his childhood when, like all Kindar children, he had been carefully taught to avoid any rough and uncontrolled activity that might lead to pain or frustration, and thereby to unjoyful emotions.

But there was yet another level—another reason why he found the sight and sound of the two children so disturbing. Appearing as they had, suddenly beneath his balcony, they seemed to be an omen—a vivid and unescapable symbol of the events of the past year and of the many problems yet to be resolved.

A scream of real panic interrupted the excited shrieks, and Hiro leaned forward in time to see the two children teetering on the edge of the branchpath. Gripping each other, they struggled to regain their balance, lost the struggle, and pitched forward into space. Hiro gasped, mindful of the possibility that the Erdling child might have had scant training in the use of the shuba. Leaning far out, he watched helplessly as the children fell.

Pushing himself free from his desperately clinging playmate, the Kindar boy tumbled once to bring his body into a horizontal position. Then, suddenly extending his arms and legs, he tightened the wing-panels of his shuba. The wide panels billowed and, his slight weight easily supported, he swooped briefly upwards and then began a sloping glide to the nearest branchpath. Below him the Erdling boy still fell, twisting and turning, his wing-panels flapping uselessly. He fell down and down, past flights of paraso birds, past vine thickets and branchpaths, past clustered nid-places. At last, far below, he managed to straighten his limbs at the right moment, and the panels billowed and held. When he disappeared from Hiro's sight, he was at last gliding, erratically, but slowly, towards the forest floor.

He would land unharmed and should have little difficulty finding one of the surface villages, and eventually he would be returned to his parents' home in the far-heights. But it was, indeed, to be regretted that some of the young Erdling families had moved into the heights before their children could be properly trained and prepared.

As Hiro returned to his chamber, he noticed that the lamps had not been tended, a task he usually performed immediately upon rising from his nid. Gathering the lamps, he returned to the balcony and released the now dimly glowing moon-moths and watched them hum away into the greening morning air. They had served throughout the night, their phosphorescent bodies lighting his labors, and now they were free to feed and rest. But Hiro's labors remained unfinished.

108

Sighing, he returned to his chamber and to the many problems that had been submitted to him for review. All around the chamber, spread out on immense table-boards, were a seemingly endless array of petitions, requests, complaints and protests—some hastily jotted on grundleaf, others carefully embroidered on silken scrolls, and some scrawled on the now familiar tablets of Erdling slate. It was urgently necessary for him to finish evaluating these messages and to determine which must receive the immediate attention of the Joined Council. Which, that is, posed the greatest threat not only to the long-range well-being of the planet, but to the immediate future, and the great Celebration that was barely a month away.

That they had come so far, that so many enormously shattering changes had taken place without major tragedies was, in itself, a triumph, although there were certainly many problems as yet unsolved, and great dangers still to be faced. There were still, almost daily, times when the future hung in the balance, so delicately poised between growth and disaster that the smallest thing—the carcass of a trencher bird on an Erdling hearth-fire, or the whispered use of the hated work "Pash-shan"—could plunge the entire planet into a catastrophe too terrible to be imagined.

Hiro returned to his task at the table-boards, but he had accomplished little when his bond-partner, Jorda, appeared in the doorway.

"It is far past the hour for food-taking," she said. "Will you eat and rest now, before the meeting of the Council?" Coming to him, she took his hands and pulled him down to sit beside her on a bench of woven tendril. "You will be ill, Hiro."

Shaking his head impatiently, Hiro began to deny the

truth of Jorda's warning, but an overwhelming sensation of exhaustion made him close his eyes and lean his head against the benchback. Jorda pressed her palms to his and, although he could not pense, he was vividly aware of her sharing of his weariness and anxiety.

"You are right," Hiro said. "I forget that my strength is no longer as limitless as it was in our youth hall days. You do well to remind me that I no longer have such endurance. The years have brought changes."

"It is remarkable that you have endured at all," Jorda said. "These last three years—two in exile in Erda and now these last months with so great a burden of responsibility. Any other would be dead by now, or far gone in Berry-dreaming." She rose suddenly. "Rest," she said. "I will bring food here, to your chamber."

Closing his eyes, Hiro had begun the ritual of relaxation when the door hangings were again thrust aside and Neric paced into the chamber.

"I am sorry to disturb you," Neric said. "Jorda said you were resting, but there are matters than can't wait."

Hiro looked at the taut, eager face and sighed inwardly. So much was owed to this young man, and yet— there were times when the sharp edges of Neric's convictions were bruising to those who were close to him.

"What is it, Neric?" Hiro asked.

"It concerns the crew of workmen who were promised from Upper Erda to work on the amphitheater. The citymaster promised fifty to be at the clearing by the seventh hour, and they have not yet arrived. The clearing of fern and rooftree is far behind schedule, and many of the stages and platforms are only partially completed. The wreaths and garlands can not be hung until the clearing is completed and—"

111

"Could extra Kindar workers be assigned to take the place of the Erdlings?"

"It has already been tried. But the tasks remaining are those that require the use of Erdling tools. Many of the Kindar workers are still unskilled in their use, and some even now refuse to use them."

"Refuse to use Erdling tools?"

"Yes. Because they are of metal and formed by fire. Some claim such tools are infused with evil powers."

Hiro's sigh was, to say the least, unjoyful, and would have been perhaps better described by the Erdling term "angry." "Who spreads such tales still?" he demanded. "I thought we had stopped such rumors long ago."

"Who knows? Rumors fly thicker than moon-moths at dusk. A few Kindar have injured themselves recently on the sharp edges of certain Erdling instruments, through carelessness or a lack of skill. But the rumors do not seem to arise from such logical causes."

"What would you have me do?" Hiro asked, after a moment's silence.

Neric's eyes narrowed as he recognized the impatience and weariness in Hiro's voice. "If you send a messenger to Kir Oblan, or one of the other Erdling Councilors, perhaps they could urge the Erdling workmen to report to the amphitheater."

"Perhaps. I shall see what I can do. But, as you well know, Erdlings are apt to respond to directives in their own way and at their own timing. But I shall send the message."

Neric raised both hands in a gesture of thankfulness and turned abruptly toward the doorway. Then, stopping just as abruptly, he came back, gesturing to the laden

112

tables. "How is it progressing?" he asked. "Have you been able to review all the petitions?"

"Nearly all. I have almost finished selecting the issues that must be placed before the Council today. We are to meet at the twelfth hour." He turned back to the tables, but Neric lingered near the doorway, seemingly uncertain whether to go or stay. For a time Hiro ignored his presence, hoping that there would be no more—no other crises to be faced. But still Neric hesitated. Hiro closed his eyes and breathed slowly and deeply before he turned, smiling.

"And—?"

The younger man's eyes blinked rapidly and then fell in confusion. I—I have no wish to trouble you further," he said. "And it may be of little importance. I cannot see that there is anything that can be done, but . . ."

Hiro waited.

"It concerns Axon Befal. It seems he has disappeared."

"Disappeared? How could he disappear?"

"He has not been seen for almost a month. The nidplace to which he was assigned at the time of his banishment, in the surface city of Farbelo, is abandoned. And he has not been reporting to his place of service."

"For almost a month? How is it that we have not been informed?"

"I don't know." I heard of it only through rumor, but when I spoke of it this morning to an Erdling Councilor whom I happened to meet on a branchpath, he seemed to know of it. Though he seemed to think it was a matter of no great consequence. He said that Befal had probably decided to live alone in the forest, and that it was no concern of the Council's as long as he did not return to Orbora."

Hiro nodded. "Possibly. But I cannot see Axon living as a recluse—"

"Nor I."

"Yet the same was said of Regle when he fled Orbora. And he has not returned to spread dissension as we feared he would do." Hiro sighed deeply. And so, now, there is another who has fled—to return constantly in dark imaginings."

"But surely there can be no connection, no common conspiracy. Not between Regle and Axon."

"It would seem unlikely," Hiro said. "Although they do have a trait in common—the lust for power."

"I know," Neric said. "It has occurred to me."

It was then that Jorda returned bearing a tray of food and drink, and behind her came Raamo. He approached Hiro uncertainly and offered his palms in greeting.

"You are much troubled," he said, "and I am sorry to come here to add to your worries." His dark gaze flowed outward as he pensed Hiro's exhaustion.

Hiro smiled. "I will rest soon—after the Celebration. What is it that you must tell me?"

"It concerns the banners," Raamo said. "The banners that are being hung along the great branchways, proclaiming the Celebration."

"Banners? What is it concerning banners that could be of such importance?"

Raamo's face flushed. "It will seem unimportant," he said, "but it is not. It is that some of the banners—many of them—are naming the ceremony the Celebration of the Holy Children, instead of Rejoyning, as was decreed by the Council."

Hiro turned to Neric. "What do you know of this?" he asked.

114

Neric was smiling. "But little," he said. "The official banners speak of the Rejoyning, but there are many others, prepared by guilds and societies and halls—Erdling groups as well as Kindar. You know, Raamo, the great Love and honor there is for Teera and Pomma throughout Green-sky. It seems to me only to be expected that some should wish to name the ceremony in their honor." Turning to Hiro he said, "Raamo has spoken to me concerning the adoration of the children, but I must confess that I have seen only good arise from it."

"I do not understand it in a way that can be spoken," Raamo said, "but I feel there is harm in it." Out of old habit, he held out his hands inviting Neric to try to grasp through mind-touch that which would not be captured in words. But Neric drew back. Once he and Raamo had been able to pense freely, but in recent months Neric's skill had been failing. Now he pretended not to notice Raamo's offered palms.

Jorda had been looking at Raamo with great intensity. Turning to Hiro, she grasped his arm. "Can you do anything about the banners?" she asked.

"I'm not sure. I can remind the Councilors of the true name of the Celebration and ask that that name only be used in the ceremonies and rituals—but I don't think that they will feel it wise to replace banners or demand that they be changed."

Raamo was clearly still troubled, but it was only too obvious that Hiro must have some time to rest before presiding over the Council meeting

"Come, Neric, let us go," Raamo said. "If you are going towards the public buildings, I will go with you. I would like to speak to you further."

Farewells were spoken, and the young men departed. Having eaten hastily and finished the classification of the petitions, there remained to Hiro a short time before the hour of the Council. Gratefully he gave his body to the soft comfort of his nid. Sleep came almost at once, but it was not without dreams.

CHAPTER TWELVE

"Hiro. You must wake up. It will soon be time for the meeting of the Council."

It was Jorda's voice, and it reached Hiro dimly at first, as from a great distance. For what seemed a very long time, he struggled upward towards consciousness through a thick fog of dreams. Dream images, fleeting, fading fragments, swarmed before him until, at last, his eyes opened and Jorda's anxious troubled face replaced the thronging shadows.

"You sleep so restlessly," Jorda was saying. "You turn and shake your head and cry out in your sleep.

"I was dreaming," Hiro said. "I feel as if I have been dreaming for days." Sighing, he climbed down from his nid and, reaching out for his bond partner, he drew her to him. They stood quietly for a time, encircled in each other's arms, drawing strength from the power of their communion.

"Of what were you dreaming?" Jorda asked.

"Of many things. Many things. The past, the far past, and the long months since the Rejoyning. But just as you awakened me, I was dreaming of the two children whom I saw earlier."

117

"The children? What children?"

"Two little boys. They were playing on the branch-path just outside my balcony this morning. One of them was obviously Erdling. In my dream they were again on the branchpath, playing roughly and running in circles, just as they were before and I was watching them. But suddenly—in my dream—I knew it was terribly important that I talk to them. I knew that they were going to fall, and I felt that I must talk to them before it happened. So I ran from the chamber and all the way through the nid-place, calling to them to wait, but just as I reached the branchpath, I saw them at the very edge clinging together. And then, before I could reach them, they fell—just as they did this morning."

"They really fell? Oh, Hiro," Jorda said. "The Erdling child? Do you think he was injured?"

"No," Hiro said. "I could see them as they fell. The Erdling boy clearly was not adept at gliding, but when I last saw him, he was gliding. I'm sure he reached the forest floor without injury."

Jorda sighed with relief. "It frightens me to think of them. They might as well be without wing-panels for all they are able to make use of them."

Turning away, Hiro went to the window and stood for a moment looking out into the forest distances.

"What is it?" Jorda's voice broke into his musing.

"I was thinking of Axon Befal. This morning Neric brought news of him. He has disappeared from his place of exile in Farbelo. It seems that he has been gone for some time, and the Erdling guards who were assigned to him did not report his absence to the Council."

"But why? Why would the guards fail to report his absence?"

118

"Who can say? Perhaps they feared they would be blamed. The Erdling Councilor to whom Neric spoke seemed to think it was only because they felt it was of little importance whether Axon lived in exile in Farbelo or in the open forest, as long as he did not return to Orbora."

"But how can they know that he will not return? At any time he could come back to Orbora to—to do again what was done to Wassou."

"True," Hiro said. "At any time."

It occurred to him, suddenly, that there might be reason to believe that Axon had already returned. He had almost put it from his mind, but now he remembered a troubling thing that Raamo had told him. Raamo had spoken of how, as he was returning from visiting the new Erdling Garden, he had suddenly received a strong pensing of evil, although the area around him appeared to be deserted. Then he had seen—or thought he had—a movement in a thicket of Vine and leaf, and had leaped from the branch without waiting to see more.

At the time, Hiro had thought—had hoped, at least—that Raamo had been mistaken. But now it seemed possible, likely even, that Raamo had indeed pensed evil; an evil so terrible that, if it had succeeded it might well have meant the end of hope and the beginning of chaos. Hiro shuddered, thinking not only of Raamo, himself, but of the barrier his blood would have been between Kindar and Erdling—a barrier more insurmountable than the Root had ever been.

"It may be," he told Jorda, "that Axon has already attempted another attack."

He told her then of Raamo's suspicion that someone had been lying in wait on the high branchpath; and as

119

he spoke, Jorda's face told him that she too realized what the consequences might have been.

"What will you do?" she asked. "What can be done by the Council?"

"I don't know," Hiro said. "I will, of course, bring up the matter in the meeting today. Perhaps there is no cause for worry. Perhaps the Erdling guards are right and Axon has only gone to live in the open forest. Let us resolve to trouble ourselves no more until we know there is reason."

But a few minutes later, when the messengers had arrived to carry the scrolls and tablets to the assembly hall, and Hiro was ready, dressed in the green shuba of a Councilor, with the gold seal of the Chief Mediator about his neck, he turned back suddenly to his bond partner.

"Jorda," he said urgently. "Perhaps this warning is needless, but it might be best if you left the nid-place only during the hours when the branchpaths are full of people—and do not go into the midheights or near the open forest. It has occurred to me that if the Nekom would contemplate attacking Raamo, who never was a Geets-kel, there may be no way of knowing the direction their vengeance will take. Perhaps they are plotting against all who are active in the Rejoyning."

Jorda's eyes widened with fear. "Genaa," she said. "Then Genaa, also, could be in danger."

"I will see Genaa at the Council," Hiro said. "I will speak to her." Pressing his palms to Jorda's and muttering the short form of the parting, he hurriedly left the nid-chamber.

His route to the Council Hall lay along the great branchways of the city, across the wide reaches of Broad and Grandgrund. At this hour, soon after midday, the branchways were crowded with people. There were many greetings. As he passed, people spoke to him, calling out, "Joy to you, Councilor," or "May your Spirit be blessed, Chief Mediator."

Although all the passers-by were shuba clad, it was apparent that there were many Erdlings among them. Hiro found himself looking for the clues: a difference in skin tone, a stocky build, an uncommon hair style. When he realized exactly what he was doing, a cold foreboding washed over him. Not for the looking itself, but for how he was looking—with fear and suspicion. If his suspicions concerning Axon—and at this point they were only suspicions—could so influence him, what would be the reaction of the other Councilors, of all the Kindar? What would be the effect on the Rejoyning if it became known that Erdlings had tried to take the life of Raamo, who had become almost as much a symbol of faith and hope as the holy children themselves.

Hiro reached the hall in an agony of indecision: should he immediately bring up the matter of Axon's disappearance or wait, in hope that it would be revealed —as it should be—by an Erdling Councilor? And should he speak at all of the possibility that the Nekom had attempted to attack Raamo? Finally, as the last group of Erdling Councilors arrived, he came to a partial decision.

He would not at once bring up the matter of Axon's disappearance. According to Neric, some of the Erdlings had known of it for some time; and properly, it would be their duty to inform the Council. Perhaps the Erdlings would speak to the Council concerning Axon's flight from Farbelo, and it was possible that they might even

121

have a solution. Just possibly, too, something might happen that would make it unnecessary to speak of his suspicion that Axon Befal had attempted to take the life of Raamo D'ok.

The meeting was long and difficult. One by one, Hiro introduced the many problems that had been brought to him since the time of the last meeting: problems concerning fears and misunderstandings, complaints and tensions, differences and prejudices that had arisen in almost every area where there had been contact between Erdling and Kindar.

Much time passed before all these matters were introduced. When, at last, they had all been spoken of, although by no means resolved, it was time to open the discussion to the rest of the Council. Turning first to D'ol Falla, Hiro asked if she had knowledge of any other urgent matter that should be brought before the meeting.

Smiling ruefully, D'ol Falla shook her head. "I have nothing to add to your burdens today," she said. "And I would suggest that any further discussion today be limited to matters of utmost urgency. It would seem to me that the mind can stand only so much troubling in a short space of time, and I think that limit has been reached, by all of us—and most particularly, by our Chief Mediator."

All around the long table-board, heads nodded in agreement, but it appeared that many matters of utmost urgency remained to be dealt with. Or perhaps it was simply that life in Green-sky had reached the point where every problem was urgent, in that it might, at any time, grow into a great and uncontrollable blossoming of evil. It was the fear of such blossoming that had

122

haunted the dreams of many for months, and that had driven Hiro on far past the point of human endurance.

It was his daughter, Genaa, who spoke next, of a matter that she had brought before the Council several times before, but for which there had been no solution. It concerned the spreading use of the pavo-berry, not only by the Kindar, but more recently in Erdling communities as well. Daily, more and more victims of the addictive berry were being brought to the healing centers. Some weeks earlier, crews of workmen had been sent out to destroy every pavo-vine in the forest around Orbora, but now it seemed that berries were being brought into the city from distant sources. Genaa asked the Council to investigate these sources and put an end to the deadly trafficking. The Councilors who had been in charge of the pavo-vine work crews agreed to renew their efforts, and the discussion passed to other matters.

Neric had been indicating for some time that he wished to be recognized. If called upon, there could be little doubt that he would bring up the disappearance of Axon Befal, and Hiro was still hoping that an Erdling Councilor would be the first to inform the Council that the Nekom leader had fled. Hesitating, Hiro noticed that Raamo, too, wished to speak.

"Raamo," Hiro said, "did you wish to address the Council?"

It was not often that Raamo spoke before the Council, and even now he seemed hesitant, uncertain.

"I don't want . . . I know it will seem unimportant . . . when there are so many problems, but will you mention to the Councilors the matter about which I spoke to you this morning? Will you ask the Councilors to remind the people about the banners, the banners that are being

123

hung in honor of the Celebration? Will you remind them that the banners should proclaim the Celebration of the Rejoyning—and not the holy children?"

Around the table-board people glanced at one another, and there were smiles and lifted eyebrows. It was clear that no one took the warning very seriously, and yet there was among the Councilors much Love and respect for Raamo, and no desire to hurt or embarrass him. It was D'ol Falla who spoke at last, and her mind was open and unblocked so that Raamo could pense that her words spoke fully of her meanings, with no secret thought beneath them.

"Raamo," she said, "we have all heard you speak before of your feeling that there is danger in the peoples' tendency to idolize Pomma and Teera and the miracle they produced on the day of the Rejoyning. As you know very well, I have great faith in your gift of Spirit and in the truth of your instincts. And I think that I can understand what it is that you fear—at least in part. I can see that your sister and Teera are very young to bear such a burden of responsibility. We who were once Ol-zhaan have reason to know that honor and glory can be very dangerous. Like you, I would wish to spare the children from all such perils, but I am beginning to wonder if it will be possible."

Then Neric burst in eagerly. "D'ol Falla speaks the truth, Raamo. Your concern for your sister and Teera is natural. They are young, it is true, but I think they are mature beyond their years. Only yesterday, when I was at the palace, I spoke to them, and it seemed to me that their responsibilities to the people and to the Rejoyning is of great concern to them."

"Neric!" Raamo said. "Neric! What did—"

But suddenly Hiro's patience was exhausted, and he interrupted bluntly. "Raamo! Neric!" he said. "There is no longer time for such discussions. "What we have heard here today makes it clear that our problems are daily growing more dangerous. The Root is dead, but the evil that it started no longer needs a Root in order to flourish. I think the time has come when we must use the children in whatever way we can if Green-sky is going to survive. I am afraid, Raamo, I am terribly afraid, that the children are our only hope. We must have faith of some kind, and the people have put their faith in the children. They alone unite us."

No one looked at Raamo, or if they did, they quickly turned away. Instead, they looked to the Chief Mediator, agreeing with him and asking that assemblies and processions be planned, at which the children could be seen and honored. A Kindar Councilor suggested that the newsingers could be given statements, made by the children, exhorting the people to forget their fears and differences and work together for the good of all. Several Erdling members urged that the children be taken in procession to all the surface cities—perhaps daily, at least for a while.

"I'm sure it would make a great difference," one of the Erdling Councilors said. "There was, in the beginning, so much hope, so much faith in the children, among our people. I'm sure that if that faith could be renewed and encouraged, it would erase many suspicions and resentments."

Hiro D'anhk acknowledged the speakers and listened to their suggestions without commenting. He found that he did not, in truth, know what he wanted to say. There was a part of his mind that held back with a cold weary

125

denial of all that was being said. A part of that denial came, he knew, from the fact that no Erdling had as yet spoken of the disappearance of Axon Befal, and another part came from the protest written on Raamo's face. But at the same time he felt a great desire to forget all doubt and denial and go with the great wave of enthusiasm and hope that was sweeping the Council.

It's true, he told himself. The people's faith in the children may still save us. They truly are our last hope.

It was then, no more than a few minutes after Hiro had conceded that there was no hope except in the faith inspired and symbolized by the holy children, that a figure burst through the door hangings at the far end of the great chamber and ran down the long aisle towards the Council board. It was a woman, a small Kindar woman, her familiar face made almost unrecognizable by fear and grief. A sharp thrill of fear shook Hiro as he realized that it was Hearba D'ok, the mother of Raamo—and Pomma.

"They're gone," Hearba gasped as she reached the table-board. "The children are gone."

CHAPTER THIRTEEN

For the first time in his life Hiro D'anhk knew complete despair. Once—almost three years before—when he had awakened to find himself alone in the utter darkness of the tunnels, he had known a terrible despairing fear. But even then, knowing himself to be below the Root, lost in an endless labyrinth, helpless and alone, there had still remained a tiny, unquenchable flicker of hope. But in the darkness he now knew, there was no light at all.

Clinging to the table-board for support, breathless from haste and fear, Hearba D'ok told the Council her story. Some two hours before, she had gone into the children's chambers and found them empty. For a while she had searched and called alone. Then she had summoned all the service people of the palace, and with their help, the search had been continued. Every inch of the Vine Palace had been scoured, but to no avail. The children were not there.

But something had been found that confirmed her growing fear. One of the palace women had discovered a rope attached to the outer corner of Teera's balcony. The rope was freshly woven of honey vine, and it was long enough to reach down to the next grund level below the palace.

"Every entryway has been guarded in recent weeks," Hearba said. "So whoever brought the rope must have arrived by gliding and departed the same way. But Teera cannot glide, so the rope must have been used to lower her down to someone who waited below."

"But isn't it possible that they went off on their own, on an exploration, as children will?" someone asked, but Hearba shook her head.

"The vine that was used to weave the rope does not grow in Temple Grove. Someone brought it to the palace. And whoever it was—" Hearba stopped, fighting to control her voice, "—whoever it was took Pomma and Teera away with them."

Hearba wept, then, turning her back and hiding her face in her hands, and except for the sound of her weeping, there was no sound at all. Around the table the Councilors, Erdling and Kindar alike, sat in utter silence. And at the head of the table Hiro D'anhk sat staring out across the piles of petitions, complaints, and protests that still lay before him.

After a measureless amount of time, someone, an Erdling Councilor, stood up and moving stiffly, made his way down the long aisle and disappeared through the doorway. Then one by one, the others followed. Hiro was not the last to go.

He did not think of Hearba or Raamo, nor could he have answered if he had been asked to explain his actions. He knew only that he was going to his nid to sleep. Afterwards he could remember nothing of his journey home across the great branchways. He could not remember the people he must have seen, or if they

128

had seemed to know what had happened. But by the time he awakened the next morning, all Green-sky knew.

By the next morning, it was as if the silence that had begun the night before in the assembly hall had grown and spread until it covered all of Green-sky. It was more than simply a lack of sound. It was a stillness—a stopping—and, in many ways, an ending. The branchways were nearly deserted, and those few people who were to be seen seemed to be strangely incomplete—hollow shells of humanity, without fruit or kernel. Although it was a day of full service, only a very few reported to their places of assignment. In Grundbaum and Ninegrund, in Upper Erda and distant Farbelo, the stillness reigned.

In his nid-place on the lowest level of Grandgrund, Hiro rose from his nid and performed the patterns of the beginning of a new day, but what he did seemed without meaning or reason, devoid of pain or Joy. Later he stood by the window for a long time, staring out into the rain-washed brilliance of the morning, and when the sun had almost reached mid-sky, he went out onto the branchpaths of the city. He walked first on the main-branchways, through the heart of Orbora, past the spacious nid-places of Kindar of high honor, past silk halls and public pantries, past Gardens and youth halls. There were few people on the branchways, and what few there were did not look at him, or he at them.

After a while he climbed upward to the midheights. There he walked for a long time along smaller branch-paths, among thickly clustered nid-places; but again the branches were largely empty, and what few people he passed were silent and empty-eyed. He climbed again, then, to the farheights, and made his way along narrow swaying branches, and here and there past the tiny hanging or cantilevered nid-places, which had once been occupied by the least productive Kindar and were now apt to be the dwelling places of recent Erdling immigrants.

Coming to the end of a long tapering branch that led nowhere, he turned and was starting to go back when he noticed that below him a long, open glidepath led down and down, seemingly unimpeded by branch or Vine. Without even a moment's hesitation, he leaned forward into space and began to glide. Except for an occasional raindove and once or twice a flock of paraso, the glidepath was deserted, and Hiro drifted down past the midheights, and on down towards a wide public branchway. But then, suddenly, he banked, avoiding the branchway, and dropped again, past the lowest branchlevel. Now there was no need to watch for glidepaths, for all around him there was a great openness, broken only by an occasional gigantic grundtrunk, and here and there, a twisted stand of Vine. And below him, drawing nearer and nearer, was the dense fern growth of the forest floor.

Using all the skill of a lifetime of experience, Hiro prolonged his glide by riding currents and catching updrafts, until at last, just as he was skimming only a few feet above the fern, he saw ahead of him a break in the dense green cover of the forest floor. Grays and browns replaced the green and white of fern and mushroom, and strange unnatural shapes jutted up everywhere, sharp-edged and rectangular. Sharpening the angle of his glide, Hiro came to earth on the outskirts of the surface city of Upper Erda.

And the stillness was there, too. Hiro had been in Upper Erda several times before, generally with a large group of Councilors, and he was familiar with the noisy vigor usually apparent in the crowded muddy streets. But now, just as in Orbora, very few people were to be seen, and those few seemed to be only partially present —blank-faced and distant. Like the people of Orbora, they did not look at Hiro. But Hiro had begun to look at them.

Perhaps it was the physical exertion—the walking and climbing, and then the long, free, mind-cleansing sweep of the glide—but whatever the cause, somewhere along the way Hiro had begun to wonder. It was not that his despair had lessened. There was still the numbness, the lack of pain or Joy or any shred of hope. But just as his need to know had once caused him to risk honor and security and finally freedom, it now tempted him to return from the protection of numb oblivion. He found that he was searching the faces of the passing Erdlings, trying to read what lay behind the empty eyes, asking himself if he was witnessing the stunned silence of shock and fear, or the deadly quiet of hopeless apathy. Then, quite suddenly something made him think of Raamo, perhaps the wide-set eyes of a passing child, and for the first time in many hours Hiro was aware of a purpose and a destination. He wanted to talk to Raamo.

From the heart of Upper Erda, a roadway paved with rooftree trunks led out of the city in the direction of Skygrund, the nearest of the grunds of Orbora. Along this roadway, normally crowded to overflowing but now almost deserted, Hiro hurried. In the deep shade of the forest floor, the light was already dimming, and there was a long climb between him and the Temple Grove.

The climb began at the newly built hanging stairway, which wound around Skytrunk as far as the first branch-

131

level. Crossing through the heart of the silent city, he climbed again at Stargrund by stair and ladder and finally by the temple rampway. The deep green-gold rays of sunset were staining the intricate tendril work of the palace as Hiro approached it across the central platform of the grove. Almost at a run, Hiro crossed the platform and blew weakly on the signal flute at the palace gate.

He could not fully have explained his haste. He could, perhaps, have told himself that it was caused by a concern for Raamo. There could be no doubt that Raamo would be in a state of great mind-pain. He had been anxious and troubled for many weeks and strangely threatened by something related to the children. And now that his foreboding had been vindicated, it was impossible to imagine how he had reacted.

Hiro knew, however, that it was not a desire to comfort and console Raamo that had caused his haste. Without hope there can be no compassion, and Hiro felt himself to be no longer capable of hope. He was sure that the differences and resentments would continue to build between Erdling and Kindar, and sooner or later the terror would begin. Blood would flow, the deadly circle would be joined, and the gentle Oath of Nesh-om would give way to the ancient oaths of hatred and vengeance.

But even without hope, there remained the need to know. What would Raamo see in this strange stillness that had settled over Green-sky? With his great Spirit-gifts for pensing and perhaps for foretelling also, what would have come to him through this silence? Would it be fear and apathy, or perhaps the breathless stifling stillness that comes before the storm? As Hiro waited

132

to be admitted to the palace, he admitted to himself that it was for the answers to such questions that he had come so far and fast.

At last an old serving man appeared at the gateway and led Hiro into a small reception chamber. Only a short time later, Raamo appeared. He smiled when he saw Hiro, offering his palms in greeting and then embracing him.

"I'm glad you are here," he said. "D'ol Falla sent for you earlier, and Jorda said you had gone out hours before and had not returned. I'm glad to see that you are here."

"Yes," Hiro said. "I was walking in the city and in Upper Erda. Is there any news concerning Pomma and Teera?"

Raamo shook his head. "No," he said. "There has been no word from them, nor concerning them. D'ol Falla thinks that if they were taken away by Axon Befal, or some other, that word will come to us soon. She thinks demands will be made in exchange for their safety. But as yet we have heard nothing."

The boy was troubled, clearly, but there was a calmness in him that was new and strange. He was not, as Hiro had feared he might be, shattered by grief and fear.

"Do you think that this—this abduction—is what you feared? The danger that might come to the children through the people's adoration of them?" Hiro asked.

For a moment Raamo looked at Hiro intently, but then his gaze became diffuse and inward and he seemed to retreat into himself. "No," he said at last, "—or at least, only in part. I felt that harm might come to Pomma and Teera, but there was more. As if there might be harm that could come to all the people—through

133

their love for the children. I did not—I still can not understand it. But it seems now that there is, everywhere, a difference—a great difference."

"Yes," Hiro said. "There is a difference. I have been walking throughout the city and also in Upper Erda, as I told you. The branchways and footpaths—all the public places—are almost deserted. And there is a silence. It is the same everywhere. Everywhere I went there was a strange, unearthly silence. What is it, Raamo? Are they waiting? Are they all waiting for the end?"

For a moment Raamo returned Hiro's questing stare with his intense deep-focused gaze. Then, lifting his head, as if in answer to a call, he turned away towards the windows. For a time he stood looking out into the soft darkness of first rainfall.

Hiro followed and stood beside him, but for a long time Raamo seemed unaware of his presence. At last Raamo sighed deeply and turned to Hiro.

"Yes," he said. "It is strange. It is like listening. Like a great listening."

And although Hiro tried to question him further, he seemed to know nothing more about the meaning of the silence.

CHAPTER FOURTEEN

On the same evening, and during the time that Hiro and Raamo were speaking together in the small reception chamber, in another part of the Vine Palace, D'ol Falla had returned from having spent most of the day with the parents of the missing children. It had been a day full of mind-pain, and she was very tired. There had been no formal food-takings in the palace that day, and she had asked Eudic to bring a small tray of pan and fruit to her nid-chamber. Soon after she reached her chambers, Eudic appeared at the door.

Eudic was an old man, almost as old as D'ol Falla herself, and he had been assigned to service in the Vine Palace for a great many years. Long ago he had taken on himself the responsibility for making a great many decisions that concerned D'ol Falla's welfare. There was, for instance, a great deal more food than she had requested on the tray that he was carrying.

"You have eaten almost nothing all day," he scolded as he arranged the food carefully on a small tendril table. "I've brought a small dish of mushrooms in egg sauce, and a tiny bit of nut cake, too. I made it myself.

135

That new pantry woman doesn't chop the nuts fine enough. And I will be very unjoyful if you do not eat every bit of it. Here, I will put the table near the window so you can hear the rain as you eat. There is nothing like rain-song to sooth the mind-pain of—"

His back had been to D'ol Falla as he arranged and rearranged the table, but now he turned, and she saw that there were tears in his eyes and on his wrinkled cheeks.

"The children?" he asked. "Has there been any word?"

Unable to speak, D'ol Falla only shook her head.

The old man sighed deeply. "Surely they are all right," he said. "Surely no one would harm children—such beautiful children. Everyone—all of us here in the palace who have known them—we are all . . . we have been so . . . unjoyful. . . ." His voice quavered, and Kindar-like he turned his face to hide the sight of his unjoyfulness and hurried from the chamber. When he was gone, D'ol Falla went to sit at the tendril table and listen to the soothing sound of the rain. It was a long time before she was able to swallow.

After a time, when the tightness in her throat had subsided, she ate a little. The rich nut cake, however, was more than she could manage. It was a pity, since Eudic had prepared it so carefully, but fortunately, there was a way to put it to good use. Going to the corner near the balcony, she took down a tendril cage and brought it to the table. In the cage a pair of green-backed joysingers, excited by the prospect of food, began to chirp and flutter.

"Hush now," D'ol Falla told them. "I have some lovely nut cake for you. Some lovely nut cake made by a kind old friend."

136

She was just putting the cage down on the table when a sudden realization made her heart stand still. It was much too light. Putting it down on the table, she released a hidden latch and opened a secret compartment under the floor of the cage. She could see immediately that it was gone, but she reached inside and groped frantically at the emptiness in the desperate hope that her eyes might have deceived her, but to no avail. The tool-of-violence had been stolen. Someone had taken the ancient weapon from the place she had hidden it on the day of the Rejoyning.

Hiro D'anhk had just left the Vine Palace and was crossing the central platform when someone passed him running swiftly. Glancing back at him, the runner faltered and then stopped and came back. It was a young man who served in the Vine Palace as porter and messenger. Holding up his honey lantern, he peered into Hiro's face.

"Hiro D'anhk?" he asked. "Is it Hiro D'anhk? How strange I should find you here. I have just been sent by D'ol Falla to summon you to the palace. I was to tell you it was a matter of the greatest urgency."

For only a moment Hiro allowed himself to hope that the news might be good—that he might have been summoned back to the palace to hear that the children had been found or, at least, that some clue to their fate had been discovered. Instead the summons concerned something entirely different—another threat to the future of Green-sky.

"Why was it still intact?" he demanded when D'ol Falla had told him of her terrible discovery. "On the day after the Rejoyning I asked you if the tool-of-violence had been disposed of—dismantled—rendered inoperable, and you said it had."

137

"No," the old woman shook her head. "No. I said it had been taken care of. There is a reason why it was not dismantled, why it was not dismantled years ago when all other such artifacts—relics from the ancestral planet —were destroyed. It is indestructible. The source of its destructive power is incapsulated, enclosed in such a way that any attempt to dismantle or deactify it would cause an explosion. A devastating release of power that would destroy everything for miles around."

"But why didn't you tell me? Why didn't you tell the Joined Council? Surely the existence of such a terrible threat—"

"Yes, I know. I see now that I did the wrong thing, that I should not have tried to keep its existence a secret. But at the time it seemed to me that it would be best if no one knew of its existence, at least during the troubled days that I was sure would come. I felt that if anyone was told, it should be the entire Council. And if forty-seven people were told, it would not be long before . . ." D'ol Falla shrugged.

"I see," Hiro said. "I can see now that there was good reason—but what if you had died suddenly?"

"I had prepared documents telling of its existence and whereabouts, which would have been given to you or to whomever was Chief Mediator. If I had died, the decision would have gone to the Council, but in the meantime I thought that I could bear the burden alone. But I was wrong. Wrong!" D'ol Falla clenched her frail fists and, bowing her head, pressed them against her forehead.

Hiro knew that he should try to console the old woman, but just as he had felt incapable of feeling compassion for Raamo, he now felt that his own hopeless-

ness made him unable to truly pity D'ol Falla's suffering. "Your motives were good," he said stiffly and without true feeling. "You thought to protect—"

D'ol Falla moaned harshly. "Protect," she cried. "Protect! Don't you see, Hiro? I have repeated the old crime. The same old crime of the Ol-zhaan and the Geets-kel. I tried to protect the people by withholding the truth."

Again, D'ol Falla covered her face with her hands. After a long silence Hiro said, "But if no one knew of its existence, who could have taken it? Surely no one would have found it in such a hiding place unless he were searching. Unless he knew that there was something to search for."

D'ol Falla looked up and her eyes were bleak. "There was one other who may have known that the tool-of-violence could not be destroyed. There was one other who, with me, was guardian of the Forgotten and had access to the secrets recorded in the ancient documents. I never discussed it with him, but it is possible that he knew."

"D'ol Regle," Hiro said. He did not look at D'ol Falla. He did not have to see her face to know that he was right. It was some time before he spoke again.

"Perhaps it is just as well," he said. "Perhaps it is for the best that the tool-of-violence still exists. Since yesterday I have been certain that the end is inevitable, and perhaps it is best that it come swiftly. If we have, indeed, inherited our ancestors' instinct for destruction, it may be just as well that we have also inherited the means to accomplish it with efficiency—that the suffering should be over as quickly as possible."

"Will you tell the Council?" D'ol Falla asked as Hiro was leaving.

140

"I don't know. I don't know if the Council will meet again."

"You could call an emergency meeting."

"No," Hiro said. "I doubt if anyone would come. And even if some did, it would be useless. There is nothing more that can be done."

It seemed to D'ol Falla that death looked at her from Hiro's eyes—the living death of total exhaustion of mind, body, and Spirit.

"Go home," she said, "and sleep. You are right. There is nothing more that can be done—at least, for now."

Later, lying in her nid, D'ol Falla wondered how she could have said, "at least for now." And how it was that she was still awake, thinking and planning. She, too, was exhausted, and burdened by awful responsibilities— as well as by the many years that she had lived. After a while she saw that the reason for her hope was exactly that—the long years and the fact that her life was almost over. Whatever happened, whatever the outcome for Green-sky, she, herself, would soon be at rest. Her personal involvement was almost over—and despair was a very personal thing. Therefore nothing was left for her except to go on hoping. Thinking of hope she fell asleep at last and dreamed, as she often did, of Raamo.

When D'ol Falla fell asleep, the night was already half spent; but Raamo himself was still awake. He was, in fact, sitting in the common room of a small nid-place in the farheights of Stargrund, listening to the soft song of the rain and the sound of many voices.

A few hours before, after his meeting with Hiro, Raamo had been about to return to his own chamber when Eudic had again appeared in the doorway.

"There is a Kindar woman at the palace gate," he

141

told Raamo. "She is asking to speak to you. I told her it was very late, but she insisted that I ask if you would see her."

"I will see her," Raamo had said, and a moment later Eudic returned and ushered in a large woman with a broad face and a keen and purposeful gaze.

"I am Fanya," she said. "Fanya D'onne. I am messenger for the fourth fellowship of the Ny-zhaan, and I have been sent to ask if you will attend our meeting. It is a special meeting called to discuss the abduction of the children, and it is, even now, in progress."

The woman offered her palms in greeting, and with palm- and eye-touch Raamo could pense no blocking, nor any hidden purposes, and so he agreed to go with her. On the way to the farheights, Fanya told him more concerning herself and the group of people that belonged to the fourth fellowship.

"I serve at the academy as a teacher of lute and songform," she told him. "And my bond-partner, Terin, serves as a recorder in the hall of public records. Several of the other Kindar members of our fellowship serve at the academy or in one of the Gardens. And many of our Erdling members are also teachers. Some of them serve in the new Erdling Gardens in Orbora, but a few go daily all the way to the old academy in Erda. We also have some members who are craftspeople, and a few are harvesters."

"Are there many Ny-zhaan?" Raamo asked.

"Not many. There are perhaps a dozen fellowships in Orbora, and most of them are very small. Ours is one of the largest, and our meetings are usually attended by no more than twenty; but there may be a larger number tonight. Our newsinger said that several people approached him today while he was announcing the meeting and asked if they might attend."

"I know very little about the fellowship," Raamo said. "What rituals do you follow and what are your purposes?"

"We have no rituals but the Oath of Nesh-om," Fanya told him, "and our purpose is only to talk and listen."

"Are your meetings often in the farheights?" Raamo asked. They were, at the time, climbing a narrow swaying ladder. Raamo's shuba was heavy with rain, and the strands of the ladder were slippery beneath his hands and feet.

"Quite often," Fanya said. "Since our Erdling members live in the farheights, and our meetings are held in the nid-places of members. Tonight we are meeting in the home of an Erdling member."

The common room of the nid-place was already full of people when Raamo and Fanya arrived. The air was heavy with body heat and the smell of rain-wet hair and shuba silk. At the appearance of the newcomers, everyone moved even closer together, until enough room was cleared for two more to sit down on the frond-woven floor. There were more than thirty people in the small room.

A man rose and began to speak. His broad shoulders and shaggy hair as well as the slow floating tones of his vowels immediately proclaimed him to be Erdling.

"I think we are all here now," he said. "Let us sing the oath."

It seemed strange to Raamo to hear the familiar words sung by Erdling voices. "Let us now swear, by our gratitude for this fair new land, that here, under this green and gentle sky, no man shall lift his hand to any

143

other, except to offer Love and Joy." Strange, but at the same time compelling, as if the newness was also in the meaning, making the words more than just oft-heard, familiar sounds.

After the oath, cups of juice and mead were passed, and the talking began. People talked to those sitting near them, and now and then someone stood and spoke briefly to the whole group. Tonight much of the talk concerned the disappearance of the children and the strange silence that had settled over the city. Some thought the children had probably been kidnapped by the Nekom, while others felt that it was just as likely that a disgruntled ex-member of the Geets-kel, had been responsible. A young man sitting near Raamo told him that he had been asked to attend the meeting because some of the members thought he might be able to help them understand what had happened—the disappearance and the silence. There was great concern among the members, the young man said, about the strange silence.

"Would you speak to us about the silence?" he asked Raamo.

Immediately there was a hush, and all eyes turned towards Raamo. Feeling frightened and uncertain, Raamo knew they were expecting a foretelling or at least great wisdom, and he felt incapable of either.

"I don't know," he stammered. "I do not understand the silence either. I have only felt that it is like listening—as if everyone is listening."

Around the room there were nods and murmurs, and an exchange of whispered comments, as if he had said something of great import. And suddenly he was speaking again, and this time it was as if the words came

144

to him slowly from a great distance.

"The quiet began in fear—because of suddenly losing the hope that there would be another miracle—that a miracle would come to save us. But then when everything had stopped and there was quiet, there began to be listening. I don't know yet what it means. But I think it is good because one can stand apart and hope for miracles, but to listen one must go out among the others."

The murmur of comment began again and lasted for some time, and then Fanya D'onne stood and spoke to the people of the fellowship. "It is very late," she said. "The first rain is over and I think we should all return now to our nid-places while the moons are shining."

Fanya was standing near the doorway; and when she ceased speaking, she pulled back the doorhangings. As she did so, something moved in the darkness of the entryway. Holding up a honey lamp, Fanya revealed the figure of an old man who had been sitting on the floor of the entryway and was now struggling stiffly to his feet.

"Greetings friend," Fanya said. "Come forward where you can be seen and welcomed into our fellowship."

Cringing like a frightened sima, the old man backed away, but Fanya reached out and, taking his arm, she firmly encouraged him to step into the light of the common room. Under the soft light from the honey lamps, the stranger's pale eyes blinked and his small mouth twisted nervously.

"I heard the newsinger . . ." he stammered, ". . . about your meeting. I—I thought I might want to join. . . ."

You should have made your presence known," someone said, "instead of staying outside in the darkness."

"I was afraid," the old man said. "I was afraid I might

145

not be welcome."

"All are welcome," Fanya said. "What is your name, that we might have it stitched on our list of members?"

She had released the old man's arm, and he once again started to back away. "My name is Quon," he said, just before he disappeared into the darkness.

CHAPTER FIFTEEN

Three days had passed since Pomma and Teera had disappeared from their nid-chamber in the Vine Palace, and to a casual observer it might seem that life in Orbora had returned almost to normal. The silence had slowly dissipated, like a morning ground-mist, and people had resumed the former patterns of their lives. To all outward appearances, all was as it had been before. There were, however, small subtle differences.

"It's as if we are all waiting," Neric told a small group of listeners, who had assembled in his youth hall nid-chamber. "As if everyone is content to sit quietly and wait for fate to catch up with all of us."

"What would you have us do?" It was Sard Uld, the Erdling hall-dweller, who spoke.

"I don't know exactly," Neric said impatiently. "Perhaps patrols could be formed to keep watch at the borders of the city, or even to go out and search in the open forest."

"To search for what?"

"For the community of the Nekom, of course." Neric said.

147

"If there is such a community."

"Surely you don't really doubt it. Everyone is speaking of it."

"I have heard of it," Sard admitted. "But only that someone knows someone, who knows someone else, who has certain knowledge of it. Have any of you met anyone who has seen it himself, or who knows where it might be?"

There were shrugs from the six people in the room— Neric and Genaa; the two Erdlings, Sard and Mawno; plus two other hall-dwellers, a young Kindar woman of twenty-two, and a boy of sixteen.

"And if there is such a place and if your patrol should happen to find it—what then?"

"Why, then we would demand the return of the children."

Sard smiled. "Very nice," he said. "*If* it was Axon Befal and his followers who took the children—and *if* they would hand them over to you simply because you asked it."

"What do you think the Nekom would do?" the young Kindar woman asked, her eyes widening with fascinated horror as she contemplated the possibilities. "What would they do if someone demanded the release of the children?"

Sard only shook his head, but Mawno, who had been lying across Neric's nid on his stomach, raised his head and answered, grinning mockingly.

"Something unspeakable, no doubt. After all, they are Erdlings."

"It's nothing to joke about, Mawno," Genaa said.

"She's right," Sard agreed. Seizing the edge of the nid, he jerked it upward, dumping Mawno out on the floor.

148

"Pay no attention to my friend," he said, smiling down at his fellow Erdling. "He is suffering from a common Erdling affliction known as plak-wit. He has eaten so many earth birds that his brain has begun to resemble a plak-hen's."

Scrambling to a squatting position, Mawno flopped around the floor, pantomiming the noisy hysteria of a startled plak; and even Neric joined in the laughter.

"It's all very well to laugh," Neric said when he was finally able to stop, "but this is no time for frivolity. If something is not done quickly, the time for laughter may soon be over for everyone. I don't see why there has not been an emergency meeting of the Council."

"My father is ill," Genaa said. "He has not been able to call a meeting; and when D'ol Falla sent a messenger to Kir Oblan and Ruulba D'arsh to ask if they would preside jointly over a special Council, they sent back word that they would wait for Hiro D'anhk's recovery."

"I know," Neric said, "and I am sorry about your father's illness, but decisions must be made soon—either with him or without him. For the sake of the children and perhaps for all Green-sky."

At that moment there was the sound of several voices from the hallway, just outside Neric's door. Going to investigate, Neric found Raamo talking to three young hall-dwellers.

"Raamo, come in," Neric said. "And you also."

Raamo entered, closely followed by the young Kindar, who a week earlier would certainly have avoided entering a chamber that held Erdlings as well as former Ol-zhaan. Neric wasn't sure whether the difference was due to a real change or only to anxious curiosity.

Raamo was obviously greatly troubled.

"Your parents and Teera's?" Genaa asked. "How are they?"

"They are in great mind-pain," Raamo said. "They have slept little, and Kanna Eld weeps often and will not eat."

There was a silence, and two or three of the young hall-dwellers extended their palms towards Raamo in the Kindar gesture of sympathy and pain-sharing.

"But I have been sent by D'ol Falla to speak with you about another matter. Another problem, a very serious problem, has arisen, and D'ol Falla feels that the Council must be informed of it. She tried to summon them to a special meeting, but they have refused to meet in the absence of the Chief Mediator. D'ol Falla has asked me to see if you, Neric and Genaa, could persuade the Councilors to attend a meeting this afternoon at the great hall."

Neric was already on his feet. "I don't know if the Councilors will listen to us, if they failed to heed the summons of D'ol Falla, but I will be only too glad to try. It will at least be better than doing nothing."

"Perhaps I could help." It was the young Kindar woman who spoke. "My father is Ruulba D'arsh, chief minister of the Kindar Councilors. He has not been himself since the news came of the abduction. He says that he, too, is ill, but I think it is mostly that he is depressed and discouraged. Perhaps if I talked to him, I could convince him that the Council must meet."

So it was decided that Jurra D'arsh, with several other Kindar hall-dwellers, would go to speak to Ruulba D'arsh; and Sard and Mawno would be sent to Kir Oblan.

"I am not Kir's son," Sard said. "But I have met him, and I think I might be able to convince him. At least

150

let me try first, Neric, before you bring the official summons. Then, if he agrees, Mawno and I can help in taking the message to the other Erdling Councilors."

Thus it was agreed, and the three—Neric, Genaa and Raamo—were soon left alone in Neric's chamber.

"What is it, Raamo?" Genaa asked. "What problem will D'ol Falla lay before the Council?"

So Raamo told them of the disappearance of the tool-of-violence from the secret hiding place in which it had lain since the day of the Rejoyning. And of the reasons why it had not been deactivated and why D'ol Falla had kept secret, until now, the fact that it still existed.

"Does she think it is Axon Befal who now has the weapon?" Neric asked.

"Perhaps, but perhaps not. The hiding place was skillfully made, so that there seemed to be no space for a hidden compartment. D'ol Falla thinks that it would not have been found except by someone who was searching—and knew that there was something for which to search. And there was only one other who knew that the tool-of-violence could never be destroyed."

"Regle," Neric said suddenly.

"Yes," Raamo said. "She thinks that Regle must have had something to do with it."

"But Regle hasn't been seen or heard from since the day of the Rejoyning." Genaa said. "Surely if he had entered the Temple Grove at any time, he would have been seen and recognized."

"But he might not have come himself. It is possible that he has allied himself with others."

"It hardly seems possible that he has joined with the Nekom. Axon Befal has sworn to destroy all who were once Geets-kel."

"True," Neric said, "but there are others who might

have joined forces with the novice-master. There have been several Ol-zhaan who have disappeared since the Rejoyning, and not a few Kindar as well."

"Then it might well be that it was not Axon at all who took the children, but the followers of Regle. They might have searched for the weapon and found it at the same time that the children were taken. If you remember, D'ol Falla was with us at the Council meeting at the time, and her chambers would have been empty."

"Yes," Raamo said. "That is what D'ol Falla thinks may have happened. She is very troubled."

In a short time messengers arrive at the youth hall with the news that the efforts of Juura D'arsh and the young Erdlings had been successful, and that most of the Councilors were prepared to meet at the great hall on the sixth hour. A messenger was sent on to the Vine Palace to inform D'ol Falla and the Eld bond-partners of the hour set for the meeting. For Raamo and Neric and Genaa, there was only time enough for a quick food-taking in the youth hall pantry, before setting out for the assembly hall.

A short time later, just as they were leaving the youth hall, the young Kindar woman Jurra D'arsh appeared running towards them along the branchway. Her face was pale and her eyes were wide and strange.

"Come," she cried. "Come. The newsinger—near Startrunk."

Turning, she hurried back the way she had come; and when they tried to question her, she only shook her head and hurried faster.

"The newsinger," was all she would say.

As they approached Startrunk, they could see that a crowd had gathered on the broad branchway near the

152

platform of the newsinger. The newsinger, a young man with a round childish face, seemed to have just finished his message. He was standing silently staring at the crowd, and just as silently the crowd returned his stare.

"Again. Again please, newsinger," Neric called.

For a moment the young man only looked blankly at Neric, as if unable to understand the meaning of his request. Then collecting himself with an obvious effort, he began to sing.

"A short time ago I was approached on this platform by a messenger who handed me this scroll." He was chanting rapidly, making no effort to employ the skills of melody, rhythm, and rhyme for which the newsingers of Orbora were so much admired. "The messenger was not known to me, but by his appearance it would seem that he was Erdling. The scroll was tightly bound, and by the time I had opened it, the messenger had disappeared. The message of the scroll is as follows:"

Unfurling a wide grundleaf scroll he began to chant —his voice high and harsh with emotion.

"From the Great Leader Axon Befal, to all the people of Orbora. Be it known that I, Axon Befal, with the help of many, both Erdling and Kindar, who are secret members of the Nekom, have taken into custody the children Pomma D'ok and Teera Eld. The children are being held in the forest community of the Nekom, which is well hidden and guarded by many loyal Nekom who are equipped with sharp-edged wands-of-Befal. The children will not be returned to their parents and to the people of Orbora until all the members of the Joined Council have sworn allegiance to me, Axon Befal, and all who were once Geets-kel have been seized and imprisoned, including the woman known as D'ol Falla and the traitor-

153

ous Verban, Hiro D'anhk. When this has been done, I will enter Orbora with a great multitude of my followers. The children will be restored to you and a new era will begin in Green-sky. An era of justice and order and peace and plenty for all who pledge loyalty to the leadership of the Nekom. If these things are not done in ten days time, the children will die."

"The children. The holy children," a voice cried, an Erdling voice lifted in the wild wailing chant of the Ceremony of Weeping. One by one other voices took up the cry, Kindar voices as well as Erdling. On the platform the young newsinger joined in the wailing, his round face wet and contorted.

Too stunned by what she had heard to think clearly, Genaa did not at once think of Raamo, who had been standing just beside her. And when she did, he was no longer there. Already some distance away, Raamo was on his way to the Vine Palace. As soon as he realized what the newsinger was saying, one thought possessed his mind—that he must reach the palace before word of Axon Befal's message arrived there. Although he knew there would be little he could say to comfort his parents, he felt that he must reach them before they heard of Axon's threat.

Running and climbing feverishly, he reached the rampway that led to the Temple Grove in a state of near exhaustion. At the end of the rampway he stopped suddenly to ease his breathing and, as he did so, he became aware of the sound of footsteps behind him. The footsteps paused when he did, and then came on more slowly. Whirling, Raamo found himself face-to-face with an old man.

Raamo backed away fearfully, trying to center his

mind enough to pense the man's intentions. He was only partially successful but, as the man's eyes met his, he momentarily sensed fear and a wild desperation—yet it was not the senseless ragings that had reached him that day in the mid-heights when he had almost been waylaid by the Nekom. As his own fear subsided, he suddenly realized that the thin pale-eyed face was vaguely familiar.

"I have seen you before," he said. "Somewhere—not long ago."

The old man opened his mouth as if to speak, but his lips trembled violently and for a moment no sound emerged.

"Yes, Honored One," he breathed finally in a voice so tremorous that Raamo had to lean forward in order to hear. "You saw me in the entryway of the Erdling nid-place—three days hence. I am Quon."

"Greetings Quon," Raamo said, offering his palms.

But the old man cringed away from him. "No, no," he said. "I am undeserving. I wish only to speak to you. I have been following you for three days—trying to find you alone so that I could speak to you in secret. I must speak to you, D'ol Raamo."

Raamo hesitated. "I am on my way to the Vine Palace. I must hurry."

"I must speak to you. I must. You must tell me what I should do."

"Would you come with me then? To the Vine Palace?"

Again the old man cringed away fearfully. "No, no. I can't. There is one there who must not see me. I will wait for you here. I have a hiding place, there, just off the rampway. There among the grundleaves. Will you return, D'ol Raamo, as soon as possible?"

155

"I will," Raamo promised. "Watch for me. I will return very soon."

"Please. Please do, D'ol Raamo. It is of great importance. It concerns—" Quon paused, glancing around fearfully, and then continued in a quavering voice. "—it concerns the tool-of-violence."

Raamo halted, torn with indecision, but there was really no choice. "I must go on, now," he said. "But I promise that I will return within the hour. Do you promise to wait for me?"

"I promise," Quon said. "I will wait. You won't tell anyone will you? You won't tell anyone about seeing me?"

"I will tell no one," Raamo said.

CHAPTER SIXTEEN

W hen Raamo reached the Vine Palace, he found his parents together with Kanna and Herd Eld in the common room of D'ol Falla's chambers. The moment Eudic ushered him into the room, grief and fear closed in around him like a dark shroud. D'ol Falla, seated in a high-backed tendril chair, looked as faded and fragile as a dried flower, and the others seemed also to be strangely changed, shriveled and closed by grief and mind-pain. D'ol Falla had been speaking, but as Raamo entered she turned to him, offering her palms.

"Greetings Raamo," D'ol Falla said, but there was no Joy in the greeting. Eudic hovered, obviously concerned for D'ol Falla's welfare. "You may go now, Eudic," she said; and when he had disappeared, she turned to Raamo. "We have just been speaking of the disappearance of the tool-of-violence. Were Neric and Genaa able to convince the Council that there must be a meeting?"

"A meeting?" For a brief moment Raamo had almost forgotten. "Yes, yes. The meeting. They were successful. The meeting will begin soon, at the sixth hour. A messenger was sent to tell you. She will arrive soon. But there is something that I must speak of first."

He paused. The messenger had, no doubt, stopped, too, to hear the announcement of the newsinger—and she would be arriving soon with more news than she had been told to bring. Yet it was he who must tell of the new disaster, and not she. Steeling himself to bear the sharing of pain, Raamo spoke as calmly as he could of Axon Befal's message. He told of the demands made and the promises, but he did not repeat, in exact words, the direct threat against the children's lives.

"Axon Befal said that the Nekom have taken Pomma and Teera and that they will be returned when his demands are met," he said.

There was a long silence broken only by the aching sounds of Kanna's sobs. It was Hearba who spoke first.

"I can not believe they would harm them," she said in a thin, childish voice. "The Erdlings joy in children as much, or more, than do the Kindar. I will not believe that they could harm them."

Raamo took his mother's hands. "You are right," he said. "We must not believe all that Axon Befal has said. I do not believe him."

"What is it that you don't believe?" D'ol Falla asked, but Raamo did not answer immediately. At last he started and turned toward D'ol Falla. "I—I don't know," he said. "But I know that we must not believe him."

"Did Axon Befal make any mention of the tool-of-violence in his message?" Herd Eld asked.

"No," Raamo said. "He said nothing about it. Nothing at all." The mention of the weapon caused Raamo's mind to return to the old man Quon, but at that moment an interruption occurred. Eudic appeared again in the door-

158

way, and with him the messenger who had been sent to announce the meeting of the Joined Council. She was pale and shaken.

"I have told them," Raamo said quickly. "I have already told them about the message from Axon Befal."

Clearly relieved that she did not have to be the bearer of such news, the young woman gave D'ol Falla a scroll on which was written the announcement of the meeting of the Council, and then departed. When she was gone, D'ol Falla spoke to Herd Eld.

"It is obvious that Kanna cannot be expected to attend the meeting, and I think it would be best if you stayed here with her. And since I have already told you what I have to impart to the Council, there is no need for you to be present. Raamo, will you go to the meeting or stay here with your parents?"

"I will come to the Council," Raamo said, "but not at once. Will it be all right if I arrive later? Will you tell the members that I will be there very soon?"

D'ol Falla looked at him searchingly for a moment, but she did not question him. It seemed to Raamo that she knew, perhaps pensed, something of his purpose.

"Yes," she said. "I will tell the Council. Will you call Eudic back? I will ask him to escort me to the assembly hall."

A few minutes later Raamo was again on the rampway between Stargrund and Temple Grove. He walked slowly waiting for Quon to show himself, and was perhaps halfway down when he pensed, and then heard, a summons. Climbing over the tendril network that bordered the rampway, he scrambled through grundtwigs toward a thick clump of leaf and Vine. A moment later he was again face-to-face with the old man, Quon.

The telling did not go swiftly. Having determined to tell his story to the Spirit-gifted young Ol-zhaan, Quon was equally determined that it should be told well, with no detail forgotten that might help to explain his behavior.

"I have always been a good and loyal Kindar, Honored One," he began. "I am a craftsman, a humble worker in wood and tendril. Almost a year ago, on the day that is now called the Rejoyning, I had been assigned to work on the rebuilding of a broken tendril screen in the palace of the novice-master, D'ol Regle. There, I had come to know well a Kindar serving man called Tarn D'ald. On that day, while I was working, Tarn came to me suddenly, greatly excited, and said that I was to receive a great honor. I had been among those chosen to accompany the novice-master into the forest on a mission of great importance. I was told to wait in a storage room—other Kindar serving people arrived, four in all—and then the two Ol-zhaan, D'ol Regle and a young novice, D'ol Salaat. We, all the Kindar, that is, were given many portage baskets to carry, and we began a long journey into the depths of the forest. When the journey was over, we had come to Wissen-wald."

"Wissen-wald?" Raamo asked.

"The new community founded by D'ol Regle. I stayed in Wissen-wald many days, helping to build nid-places and reservoirs. But then, several months ago, it was decided that I should return to Orbora to serve as a recruiter. I was told to go back to my old nid-place in the guild home, and to my place of service at the guild of builders. I was to say that I had been lost in the forest."

"It would seem odd that such a story would be believed. Why didn't your family report you missing?"

"I have no family, Honored One. I was bonded once, when I was young, but we were not blessed with children and we decided to break our bond and return to hall living. So there was no one to grieve at my absence. And there was so much that was strange in Orbora—so many other things to trouble about—no one seemed to have the time to question my story. So I lived again in Orbora and worked for my old guild, but while I worked I was always to talk to people—about the Erdlings and about the old days and of D'ol Regle. And when I found others who longed for a return to the safety of the days before the Rejoyning, I took them to a secret meeting place in the forest to talk to D'ol Salaat, or one of the other Ol-zhaan; and if they were found worthy, they were taken to Wissen-wald."

"But the tool-of-violence?" Raamo asked. "You said you wished to speak to me about the tool-of-violence."

"Yes, yes, D'ol Raamo. I am coming to that."

"And Quon. You should not call me D'ol."

"I know, I know, D'ol . . . I mean Raamo. But it is hard for me to remember."

"I understand," Raamo said smiling. "And now, about the tool-of-violence?"

"Yes, the tool-of-violence. What I wished to say was that there are others in Orbora besides myself, perhaps many others, who are secret members of the community and who are here on many missions. There is one whom I have met—who has reported to D'ol Salaat with me—who serves in the Vine Palace and whose mission it is to find the tool-of-violence and bring it to D'ol Salaat."

Raamo stared at Quon in horror. He knew all the serving people of the palace well, and there were none

161

whom—but then, suddenly, he knew. There was one who mind-blocked very carefully in his presence. He had, at times, wondered about it. "Maala?" he asked. "Maala D'ach?"

"Yes, yes, Maala."

"Has the tool-of-violence been taken to Wissen-wald?"

"To Wissen-wald? I don't think so. She has not found it yet. At least she hadn't found it a week ago when we last spoke to D'ol Salaat in the meeting place. D'ol Salaat was very unjoyful because it had not yet been found."

"But it is gone now," Raamo said. "Someone found it and took it away from where it had been kept, since the day of Rejoyning."

The old man closed his eyes and let his head fall forward upon his chest. When he raised it again, his pale eyes seemed to have faded even more—as bleached and lifeless as the eyes of one far gone in wasting.

"Then I am too late," he said. "He will kill them this time, for certain."

"Them? Who, Quon?"

"The children. The holy children."

"Do you think that Regle has the children, then? Was it his people who took them from the palace?"

"Yes, I am certain of it. He has taken them as he did before, that he might use them to force his will upon the people of Orbora."

"Have you heard the newsingers, today?" Raamo asked. "Haven't you heard of the message given today to the Startrunk newsinger?"

"No, I have heard no messages today. I have spent the day here in this hiding place waiting for you to cross the rampway."

Raamo nodded slowly. After a while he asked, "Quon, why is it that you no longer serve Regle? You went with him into the forest and you have served him secretly in Orbora. Why is it you no longer serve him?"

"It is because of the children," Quon said eagerly. "When I went into the forest with D'ol Regle, I had not heard about the children and of how they took away the evil power of the ancient tool of death by the holy power of uniforce. While I served in Wissen-wald, we were told a story of what had happened on the day of the Rejoyning—but it was not a true story. We were told that the children stole the tool-of-violence, but not how they took it. We were not told about D'ol Regle's threat against the lives of the children. Instead—they told us many things that were not true.

"But then, when I was sent back to Orbora, I began to hear other accounts of what had happened on the day of the Rejoyning. For a long time I was not sure what to believe. But after a time I began to see that many of the things I had been told to tell the new recruits were not true—things about the Erdlings and the Rejoyners. Still I was afraid and uncertain. I could not decide what to do.

"Then, three days ago, when I heard that the children had again been stolen, I knew suddenly what I must do. I knew then what it was that D'ol Regle planned to do, and I felt that I must stop him. I have long had great faith in you, D'ol—I mean—Raamo, since I first saw you when you were announced as a Chosen. I felt that I must speak to you. I knew that you were living at the Vine Palace, but I was afraid to go there because of Maala, so I began to follow you, hoping to catch you alone.

163

"But yesterday was the time for me to report again to D'ol Salaat in the secret meeting place, and I did not go. And since that time I have been afraid to show myself anywhere. I am afraid of everyone—because anyone might be secretly in the service of D'ol Regle. I do not dare go back to my guild hall. I am an outcast. And it is all for no purpose. I found you too late."

"Perhaps it is not too late. I know that it will be useful to the Rejoyners to know of these things—of Regle's community and of his secret followers in Orbora. But there is something that you should know. Earlier today a newsinger was given a message from Axon Befal, the leader of the Erdling group called the Nekom. Do you know of them?"

"Yes. I have heard many rumors about them."

"The message was that they have taken the children. Axon is demanding that the Council swear allegiance to him in return for the safety of the children."

A shock of surprise shook Quon. When he recovered himself enough to speak, he said, "It seems impossible. I was so certain—"

"Perhaps, now, you will decide to go on serving Regle, since it was belief that he had taken the children that made you turn against him."

Quon did not answer immediately, but when he did he said, "No, I was almost decided before I heard of the abduction of the children. And then, that night, I followed you and the Kindar woman to the farheights and waited for you in the entryway. I was able to hear much of what was said by those who call themselves Ny-zhaan. And what I heard made me see—made me understand. . . . No, I would no longer be able to go on serving D'ol Regle, whether or not he has stolen the children."

164

Quon's story was finished, and the telling left him drained and shrunken, as if he had been living on the strength of his resolve to find Raamo and speak to him, and now that the speaking was over, he was left without plan or purpose.

"Where will you go now?" Raamo asked.

"I don't know."

"I think I know a place where you would be safe and well cared for. Perhaps you could wait here until darkness and then go to the nid-place in the farheights—the one where you waited for me in the entryway. The people there are Ny-zhaan. I think you would be safe there."

A glimmer of hope returned to the pale eyes. "Yes, yes," he said. "You are right. I should have thought of it before. The woman said that all are welcome."

"I don't think you will have to worry there about secret followers of Regle. The Ny-zhaan seem to have few secrets."

When Raamo left Quon's hiding place, he hurried to the nearest glide-path and within a few minutes he was landing on the broad branchway that led past the assembly hall. When he entered the hall, he found that D'ol Falla had already finished telling the Council about the continued existence of the tool-of-violence, and the terrible fact that it had disappeared.

"There is nothing more that I can say," D'ol Falla was saying as he approached the Council-table. "I know that I have failed you and the Rejoyning. That my motives were good does not excuse me. If I had trusted the Rejoyning enough, a better way might have been devised— a better way to solve the problem. But now it is too late, and there is nothing that I can do. Except, of course, I am immediately resigning from the Council. My poor

165

judgment should bring no further harm to you and to the people of Green-sky."

The Council was incomplete. A few Erdlings and several Kindar Councilors were not in their places. And without the accustomed leadership of the Chief Mediator, Hiro D'anhk, the meeting seemed directionless and uncertain. For the moment at least, the Councilors showed little awareness of the terrible implications of the disappearance of the ancient weapon. Most of them were more concerned with D'ol Falla's grief and with her intention to resign from the Council.

For several minutes Raamo listened to one speaker after another try to comfort D'ol Falla, telling her that she was not to blame—that under the circumstances her decision to keep the existence of the deadly weapon a secret was understandable and justified. One of the speakers, a Kindar woman, turned to Raamo.

"You have not spoken, Raamo," she said. "Do you not agree with us that D'ol Falla should not blame herself and must not leave the Council?"

"Yes," Raamo said. "I do agree. But I must speak of something else. Something that concerns the tool-of-violence. I have just come from a meeting with one who has given me important information about the tool-of-violence, and about other things, also."

So Raamo told Quon's story to the Council, taking care to leave out no detail concerning Regle and his community of Wissen-wald and of his secret spies and the woman Maala D'ach, who had been given the task of stealing the weapon. When he had finished, D'ol Falla was the first to speak.

"Yes," she said. "I see now that it must have been Maala who found the hiding place."

166

Neric was on his feet. "Why are we sitting here wasting time," he said. "Let us immediately go to the palace to bring this woman before the Council. Ruulba, will you go with me to summon the traitor, Maala D'ach, to appear before us?"

But D'ol Falla was shaking her head.

"It is useless," she said. "For two days Maala has been absent from her duties at the palace. It seems she has already gone to this new city of Regle's, this Wissenwald, with the weapon. It would seem that we now have two who have gained the means to threaten us into submission. Axon Befal has the children, and Regle again has the tool-of-violence."

CHAPTER SEVENTEEN

J ust as the news of the abduction of the children had spread over Green-sky with great swiftness, so too did the incredible facts concerning Axon Befal's demands and the stolen tool-of-violence. But this time, instead of a silence, there was a great increase in conversation. People gathered everywhere—in guild halls and nid-places, at places of service and on the public branchways—and talked about the two secret cities hidden somewhere in the open forest; about the woman Maala D'ach, and her treachery; and about the terrible threat of the tool-of-violence, once more in the hands of Regle.

The tool-of-violence was, perhaps, the most discussed of all. A year earlier, the people of Green-sky had been intrigued and horrified to learn that such a device existed. In the intervening months a new mythology had grown up around the ancient weapon, based partly on fact, but largely on surmise—a mythology that covered its appearance, its history, the terrible deeds it had once performed, and the source and extent of its awful power. This new mythology had made of the ancient weapon a symbol of evil that their ancestors had escaped by flight, but which pursued them, only to be conquered by the power of uniforce and of the Rejoyning.

That it had been conquered, they had not doubted, since it was assumed that it had been destroyed after the Rejoyning. And now, to learn that it still existed, and that it could not be destroyed, transformed the triumphant myth into one of almost fatalistic fear—a fear that the curse of violence was indeed unconquerable, and that the tool itself was the physical manifestation of a hidden evil that still lived and moved among them. They spoke of it during the day with superstitious awe, and during the night it became the nightmare monster of their dreams—a thing of living, knowing evil, forever willing the return of its ancient power over life and death.

In the great assembly hall, the Council, also, talked. The Councilors present at the meeting at which the new revelations had been made had decided to meet again in two days time, and every two days thereafter until a solution had been found. By the first such meeting Hiro D'anhk had recovered enough to resume his duties as Chief Mediator, and even the grief-stricken parents of Teera had returned to their places at the table.

The Council had sent a message to the Citizens' Senate in each of the seven cities, as well as to the city-masters and clan-leaders of Erda and all the surface cities. The message asked that representatives be sent to inform the Councilors of how the people felt about the threats of the two renegade leaders.

The representatives had begun to come, but they brought few suggestions as to what should be done. There was, however, general agreement on what should not be done. Very few, it seemed, thought that the Council should ransom the children by swearing allegiance to Axon Befal, and even fewer advocated an attempt to rescue them by means of force. It seemed clear to both Kindar and Erdling that either solution would be a denial of the children—a denial perhaps more final than their deaths. To most, it seemed that no answer was possible, and all that could be done was wait and hope— hope that Axon Befal and Regle D'orte would not be capable of the evil they had threatened, or that the power once before manifested through the children would somehow keep them and all Green-sky safe from harm.

And so the waiting continued. In the Vine Palace, D'ol Falla also waited, through days that had become, for her, eternities of torment. She waited in constant expectation of the news that Regle had presented his demands to the Council—demands based on the power of the stolen weapon—or that a message had arrived from Axon Befal, a message, perhaps, that he was advancing on the city.

Just as she had done before when disaster seemed imminent, she fell back on her faith in Raamo. Summoning him into her chambers, she urged him again and again to seek for Spirit-guidance. But, just as before, Raamo was unable to summon a foretelling.

"I've tried," he told D'ol Falla, "but there is no answer."

"Perhaps you have not tried hard enough," D'ol Falla said. "Perhaps if you spent more time in seeking—in fasting and in meditating. You have often been gone from your chambers in the last few days. Where have you been and what have you been doing?"

"I have been to the youth hall, and now and then to meetings of the Ny-zhaan."

170

"Do you feel, then, that the Ny-zhaan have discovered answers to our problems?" D'ol Falla said with some impatience. "Answers that the Council is not capable of discovering, or that you might not find in foretelling if you spent the time in fasting and ritual?"

"I don't know. I have heard little concerning answers at their meetings. But they are seeking."

"Many others are seeking," D'ol Falla said. "We are all seeking. But I feel that there is no hope of an answer except through the Spirit, and in the past the Spirit has spoken through you."

Raamo would only shake his head. His reaction puzzled D'ol Falla. He seemed preoccupied and strangely calm. Earlier, when the dangers had been so much less urgent and serious, he had been violently distressed; and now, with even the life of his beloved sister hanging in the balance, he seemed to have retreated into a calm denial of the truth. There were times when she almost wondered if he were Berry-dreaming. She wondered, too, if the Ny-zhaan were in any way responsible for his inexplicable behavior. It was on the sixth day after Befal announced his capture of the children that Raamo arrived at the Council meeting with a message from the Ny-zhaan—a message that several of the fellowships of Orbora had organized searching parties and sent them out into the forest to seek for the children and for the secret communities. There was much consternation in the Council.

"But what will they do if they find the Nekom or Regle's city?" Hiro D'anhk asked. "Surely they would not be so foolish as to approach them."

"I think they were planning only to observe them," Raamo said, "without making their presence known."

"But what if they are seen? They may be attacked themselves and destroyed; and that might well start the destruction of all Green-sky. I feel that it is the duty of the Council to advise these searching parties to give up their plans and remain in Orbora."

The Council seemed to be in agreement with Hiro. There was much nodding of heads and many gestures of support.

"I think . . . I am afraid that it is too late," Raamo said. "The search parties have already set out. By now they are far into the forest. I am sorry. I did not know that they planned to set out before the Council was notified or I would have advised them to wait for your approval."

There was little that could be done. It was agreed that other searchers would be sent to look for the Ny-zhaan parties, to warn them of the danger and to urge that they return immediately to Orbora. But there was little hope that all of them could be found in time.

On the tenth day, the day on which, according to the message of Axon Befal, the children were to die if his demands had not been met, there was great unjoyfulness in Orbora. People spoke solemnly in hushed voices, and greetings were made with tears instead of smiles. Outside the Vine Palace a great crowd of people gathered on the central platform of the Temple Grove. The crowd, composed of both Erdlings and Kindar, sang softly. At times they sang Kindar hymns of peace and comfort, and at others they chanted dark, grief-filled Erdling songs of exile. Throughout the long day, as some left the crowd, drawn away by duty or responsibility, new arrivals took their places, and the singing continued.

When night came and the first rain began, an old

172

serving man appeared at the entryway of the palace and asked the singers to come into the great hall. There, under the vaulted ceiling of the ancient palace, the old songs echoed and reechoed, until their soft sounds became as continuous and soothing as the murmur of forest rain-song.

Throughout the next day and the next, the people of Orbora waited in constant expectation of disaster. If a newsinger appeared on a branchway, he was immediately surrounded. In fact, wherever people were gathered, the entrance of any new arrival caused heads to turn in fearful expectancy. Anyone, at any moment, might be the bearer of the dreaded tidings: that the children were certainly dead, that Regle had made known his plans for the future of Green-sky, to be enforced by the tool-of-violence. But no word came, and the hours passed and the days, and the people went about the daily pattern of their lives, because it made the waiting easier to bear.

Almost a week had passed since the day given by Befal as the time the children would die if his demands were not met, when the first of the Ny-zhaan search parties returned to Orbora. It was a small group, only five men and two women, and they made their way to the nid-place of Hiro D'anhk without attracting attention. There they spoke for sometime to the Chief Mediator and then were sent home to their nid-places to rest, with instructions to be present at the Council meeting on the following day.

Raamo arrived at the assembly hall the next morning in a state of great excitement. He had been told that a search party had returned, but nothing of what information they would have for the Council. But he felt certain

173

that there would be news of great importance. One of the members of the search party was Quon, who had once served in Wissen-wald and knew its location.

As Raamo had discovered before, Quon's stories were not told quickly. His obvious nervousness did not prevent him from telling of the search with proper thoroughness and deliberation. He told first of how the group had taken more than two days to reach Wissen-wald by a roundabout route, to avoid a chance meeting with an inhabitant of the community.

Then, when they were very near, they had climbed high and approached the community from the farheights, advancing slowly through thickets of endbranches until they were able to see the roofs of the highest nid-places. There they had waited while Quon went on alone, climbing lower with extreme caution, until he had reached a hidden vantage point from which he was able to observe the comings and goings along the main branchpaths of the community.

"But there was little to see," Quon told the Council, his pale eyes blinking rapidly with nervousness. "The buildings were there, the nid-places and the public pantry, just as I myself helped to build them. But the people —either many of the people have gone elsewhere, or they were staying shut up in their nid-places from morning 'til night like a bunch of nightflyers. For two whole days I watched the main branchpaths, and in all that time I saw only four people—or perhaps it was only three."

"And who was it that you saw?" Hiro prompted.

"Well, I saw D'ol—that is, Regle himself, I'm sure of that. You couldn't mistake the size of him. And one other Ol-zhaan. I think it might have been the young

174

Ol-zhaan, D'ol Salaat. That is, he still calls himself D'ol Salaat, Councilor."

"And no other Ol-zhaan?"

"No others."

"How many Ol-zhaan were there at Wissen-wald when you were last there, Quon?"

"Well, I hadn't been back there since I was sent to Orbora as a recruiter, so it was some months ago. But at that time there were eleven or twelve Ol-zhaan, and more than three times that many Kindar. But I think they must have built a new community someplace else. Otherwise I'd have seen more and heard more. The place was as quiet as moonshine, Councilor. And no one on the branchpaths except Regle and the one other Ol-zhaan, and now and then one Kindar. I think it might have been Tarn D'ald, or that friend of his who is called—Pino, I think it is, Councilor."

"And there was no sign of the tool-of-violence?"

"Well, I don't know if I'd know a tool-of-violence if I saw one, Councilor. But the only person I saw carrying anything was the Kindar when he went back and forth between Regle's nid-place and the public pantry. And from where I was, it just looked to me as if he was carrying eatables—and not a whole lot of that."

So the meeting ended with no great revelations and only deepening bewilderment, although Raamo felt that there was a significance to Quon's story that had not yet been understood. Within the next few days, other search parties returned, and new and larger groups went out into the forest. Soon the return of search parties became almost a daily occurrence, and every meeting of the Council was at least partly devoted to hearing their reports. But there was strangely little to be told.

175

Other groups had found the city of Wissen-wald, and their reports were much the same as Quon's. D'ol Regle had been seen and two or three others, but the rest of the community were not in evidence.

One searching party, scouting far to the southwest of Orbora, had located the deserted remains of a small surface camp. Too small and makeshift to be called a city or even a community, it might have been, the searchers thought, an outpost of the Nekom. The remains of hearthfires, as well as the style of construction, indicated that it had been built by Erdlings; and a Nekom emblem —a curved knife mounted on a long staff—had been found in one of the roughly built shelters. But, although the area for many miles around had been thoroughly searched, no sign was found of the headquarters of the Nekom. Nor did any of the searching parties bring back the slightest clue as to the whereabouts of the children.

As the days passed, the searching parties ranged farther and farther afield. The forest was scoured, grund-leaf by grundleaf, not only around Orbora, but also in the vicinity of each of the other seven cities, while below the forest floor, teams of Erdling searchers ranged through the caverns and tunnels of Erda. It began to seem that a dark hole had opened somewhere in space and had swallowed up a large number of people—all of the Nekom, most of the followers of Regle, as well as the two children who had come to represent the last hope of the people of Green-sky.

CHAPTER EIGHTEEN

Seated at the head of the council table in the assembly hall, Hiro waited and thought back over the events of the past year, struggling against an un-Kindar-like feeling of bitterness. Almost twenty days had passed since the disappearance of the children, and the strange illness of the Spirit that had stricken him at that time had receded, but it had left him subject to sudden fits of depression. The depression deepened as he considered how few days remained before the Celebration, and how little had been done in preparation for it, since the children had been abducted.

In the last twenty days there had been no time to even consider the vast number of petitions, protests, and complaints that had once seemed urgently in need of arbitration. They had been pushed aside and all but forgotten. And none of the final decisions as to ceremony—what rituals would be performed, traditions observed, and personages honored—had been made. Now and then a Councilor would mention the need to move forward with the plans for the Celebration, and there would be general agreement, but a more pressing matter would soon intervene, and the suggestion would be forgotten. There was, Hiro thought, a kind of relief in the forgetting. For the moment at least, they were not forced to acknowledge a painful conviction shared by all—a conviction that the last day of the year of the Rejoyning would arrive without bringing anything that would give cause for celebration.

There were, however, some preparations that had continued to move forward. On the floor of the forest, just to the south of the city of Orbora, the great new amphitheater was nearing completion. Driven, perhaps, by the need to forget their fears in hard physical activity, the Erdling work crews had begun to labor prodigiously. In the absence of directives from the Councilors, Erdling craft-masters and clan-leaders had been directing their traditionally independent and unregimented workers with results that surprised Erdling and Kindar alike. Rank on rank of benches, huge platforms, and soaring stages had appeared in an amazingly short time, while overhead, Kindar craftsmen had almost completed the elaborate decorative arches of woven tendril.

Throughout Green-sky, other craftsmen, both Erdling and Kindar, had continued to work on tasks that were related to the Celebration. In the silk halls of Orbora, weavers and embroiderers were completing banners and tapestries destined to decorate the streets and branchways. And in the craftcaves of Erda, workers in precious metals were producing hundreds of pendants decorated with engraved representations of the palm-joined hands that symbolized the Rejoyning.

Hiro found himself brooding darkly on the irony of all this. Earlier, when there had been great reason to hope and much to work for, the people had occupied

178

themselves with dissatisfactions, suspicions and antagonisms. And now—now when the knives of the Nekom, and the death-dealing relic in the hands of Regle, hung heavy over their heads and when the beloved children who had inspired the faith that had made the Rejoyning possible had disappeared; now when hope itself seemed a foolish and idle affectation—the people worked peacefully and with great industry to prepare for a celebration that had lost all reason for being.

Hiro was roused from his unjoyful musings by the arrival of the first group of Councilors. The meeting would soon have to begin, and at this meeting, only eight days from the appointed time, there could be no further postponement of the decision that had to be made concerning the Celebration. Today the Councilors would have to face painful truths and decide whether to cancel the Celebration or to proceed with a form and ceremony that was now without reason or meaning.

The Councilors began arriving steadily, in groups of two or three. Genaa entered with Neric, and for a moment, Hiro's heart was lightened by the sight of his beautiful daughter. Then D'ol Falla arrived, leaning on Raamo's arm. The old woman, more frail and withered daily, but lit by the undiminished fire of her strange green eyes—and Raamo, whose childlike, deep-eyed gaze seemed to be less and less able to focus on the harsh facts and forms of reality.

Then came Kanna and Herd Eld, pale and silent in their grief for their lost child, and the Council was complete. When all were seated at their places around the table, Hiro greeted them, forcing his lips to smile, although Raamo at least, and perhaps others, would know that his smile was without substance.

179

"My greetings, Councilors," Hiro had said, and suddenly he ceased speaking, his attention diverted by a lone figure that was slowly approaching the council table. Moving hesitantly and uncertainly down the long aisle, the woman stopped once and half turned, as if almost deciding to retreat, back the way she had come. She came on again slowly, then, her head bent low over what seemed to be a grundleaf bundle that she carried clutched against her chest. Her thick graying hair hung in long uncombed strands, and her shuba was torn and stained. She had almost reached the table when someone whispered, "Maala. Maala D'ach."

Her head flew up, and Hiro could see that it was, indeed, Maala D'ach, the woman who had served at the Vine Palace, while secretly following the orders of Regle, until she, too, had vanished.

"Yes, it is I, Maala D'ach," the woman said. "I have decided to come back and tell you what I have done."

"As she spoke, the woman's head sank lower, her eyes darting fearfully away from the staring eyes of the Councilors. Her voice faltered, and she swayed on her feet as if about to fall.

"Be seated," Hiro said. "You seem to be ill or very tired."

A Councilor sprang to his feet and brought forward a chair, but Maala shook her head fiercely. "No," she said. "I will stand. I will stand until I have finished with what I have to tell." For a few moments she stood breathing deeply as if gathering her strength and courage, and then she began to speak.

"I am Maala D'ach," she said again, her voice becoming stiff and monotonous as if she had determined what she would say at an earlier time, and was now quoting from memory. "I served D'ol Falla at the Vine Palace. But when the Rejoyning came, and all the changes, I was fearful and often wished for things to be as they had been before. Then one day an old friend approached me, a man who had long served in the palace of the novice-master, D'ol Regle. This man, who is called Wuul, told me that D'ol Regle had started a new city in the forest, where there were no Erdlings and everything was just as it had been in the old days. My friend asked if I would like to go there, and I said that I didn't know. I feared the Rejoyning, but I feared D'ol Regle also, because he had stolen the children and threatened their lives with a tool-of-violence. The children had come to live in the Vine Palace, and I knew and loved them, as did all who knew them. But Wuul told me that it was not true that D'ol Regle had threatened the children. He said that it was a lie told by the Rejoyners to hide their own evil intentions. So I believed Wuul, and I said that I would like to go to live in D'ol Regle's city.

"Then, one day, I was taken by Wuul to a secret meeting place in the forest where I spoke with an Ol-zhaan. Not D'ol Regle, but a young Ol-zhaan called D'ol Salaat. And D'ol Salaat told me about the city of Wissen-wald, how beautiful it was and how safe, and how I would soon be allowed to go there to live. But not at once. He said that I could not go at once because first there was a task that I must perform."

Maala's head dropped lower, and her voice faltered and died away. When she began to speak again, it was so faint that some of the Councilors who were farthest away had to move closer in order to hear.

"I did not want to do the task," she said. "But D'ol

181

Salaat assured me that the evil things said of D'ol Regle were not true, and that it was D'ol Falla who planned to use the tool-of-violence against the Kindar unless they would become as Erdlings—fire worshippers and eaters of flesh. And so I believed D'ol Salaat, and I began to search through the entire palace. I even stole the key from D'ol Falla while she slept and searched through the room called the Forgotten, but it was not there. Then, one night while D'ol Falla was at the evening food-taking, I searched again in her nid-chamber and I found it, in a secret place beneath a cage of joysingers.

"I would have taken it that night to D'ol Regle, but I had not yet been to Wissen-wald and I did not know the way. So I hid it, to wait for the time when I was next to meet with D'ol Salaat in the secret meeting place. But then, before the time came for the meeting, the children were taken from the palace and I heard D'ol Falla weeping."

Maala paused again, and when she continued her voice was choked and thick. "I loved the children. All who served in the palace loved them. And when they were gone and I saw that D'ol Falla wept, I feared that D'ol Salaat had lied to me and it was true that it was D'ol Regle who had threatened the children. And I thought that perhaps he had stolen them again, that he might try again to harm them. So I wanted to return the terrible thing that I had taken—but then, I was not sure. I was not sure who had been lying and what would be done to me if it was known that I was the one who had taken it.

"Late at night, I decided to return it, and I took the thing from its hiding place and ran to D'ol Falla's chamber, but when I got there she was not alone. I could

hear voices through the door-hangings, and they were speaking of the tool-of-violence and how it had been taken. Suddenly I was terribly afraid, and I ran back to my own chamber and gathered a few things together, and then I ran away into the open forest. I have been alone in the forest ever since."

"In the open forest?" Hiro asked. "How is it that you were not found by the searchers?"

"I ran before them," Maala said. "It is possible to stay ahead of the searchers if you stay constantly alert. You wait and listen and when you hear them coming, you run before them."

"But what did you do with the tool-of-violence while you were hiding in the forest?"

"I will tell you. I have come to tell you. But first I must tell you why. You see, I didn't know until two days ago about the Nekom leader—that he had sent a messenger to say that he had taken the children. I had spoken to no one, and so I didn't know. But then two days ago I met someone. I found myself suddenly face-to-face with one who had been traveling as fast and quietly as I, so that I had no time to hear his approach and flee. And the man was Wuul, the same friend who had asked me to serve D'ol Regle. And so I spoke with Wuul, and I learned many things.

"I learned that Wuul had gone to live in Wissen-wald many weeks before, but that now he had ceased to serve D'ol Regle and was on his way back to Orbora. He said that D'ol Regle had become a Berry-dreamer—that he had become addicted to the pavo-berry and had become ill and demented—and that all his followers had left him. It had happened, Wuul said, when D'ol Regle's informers brought word that the Nekom had taken the

184

children and that the tool-of-violence, also, was missing. D'ol Regle was certain that Axon Befal had the tool-of-violence, and the thought was more than he could bear. For days he ranted and trembled, and then he began to eat pavo-berries. He refused to see anyone except D'ol Salaat and one or two of his old serving men. So one by one everyone left Wissen-wald. Most of them went to Paz or Farvald, where they would not be known, but Wuul, himself had decided to return to Orbora.

"When Wuul had gone, I could not decide what to do. I wanted most of all to help the children—to help to save them from the Nekom. At times I was sorry that I had not taken the tool-of-violence to D'ol Regle, and that I had unjustly suspected him of taking the children. But now it was too late, since according to Wuul, he was demented and addicted to the berry of death. So, at last I began to see that I must come here. I began to see that, whatever happened to me, I had to return to Orbora so that the tool-of-violence could be used against the Nekom to make them return the children."

As she spoke, Maala D'ach placed the grundleaf bundle that she had been carrying on the table-board and began to untie its bindings. As the bindings fell away, one by one, the shaking hands of the woman folded back the layers of leaf, and the Councilors leaned forward, staring. The silence deepened until the surrounding air seemed drained, even of heartbeat and breath-flow.

Except for the seven who had stood before that blunt snout on the day of the Rejoyning, no one in the hall had ever seen the ancient weapon before or anything even remotely like it. All around the table the Councilors stared in horrified fascination at the incredible artifact— a tool devised and designed, shaped and charged, for the sole purpose of destroying human lives. The thought, like the strange shape before them, was utterly obscene.

"Look! Look to Maala!" It was D'ol Falla who spoke, rousing the Councilors from their horror; and those nearest the serving woman turned to see her reeling backwards, her hands pressed against her mouth, her face as white as tendril.

A chair was hastily placed, and supporting hands guided the half-fainting woman into it. Her hands and feet were massaged, and after a few minutes she seemed somewhat recovered.

"What is it, Maala?" D'ol Falla asked. "Are you ill? Have you gone without eating?"

"I—I—have eaten little," Maala said. "But it is not that. It is that—the tool. I have carried it bound to my back since I ran away into the forest. I was afraid to leave it anywhere, for fear it would be found. So I bound it to my back. It has been there night and day like a curse. I could feel it constantly, through the pack and grundleaves—cold and heavy and evil. I can still feel it there—like a wound."

Someone brought a goblet of honeyed water, and Maala drank; and after a time she seemed calmer and not quite as pale. Genaa had come to sit beside her, putting her arm around the woman's trembling shoulders.

"Councilors," it was Raamo who was speaking, and the Councilors turned to look at him in some surprise. The boy seldom spoke in Council unless he was questioned, and never without recognition by the Chief Mediator. But now he had sprung to his feet, and his voice trembled with intensity.

"I have thought about this thing—this tool-of-violence —for many, many days. I have thought about what

186

could be done if it should be found. I know that it is impossible to take away its power, but it seemed to me that there must be a way to rid ourselves of it—to free Green-sky from its power.

"And a thought came to me, a thing that could be done. I have heard that, in Erda, there is a distant cavern that ends in a deep crevice, and far below the crevice there is a lake. A lake so deep that there is no way to measure its depth. It is called the Bottomless Lake, and nothing that falls into it will ever be recovered." Turning to the Erdling Councilors, Raamo asked, "Is it true that such a place exists?"

"It is true," Kir Oblan said. "Many generations ago a workman fell into the lake, and it was probed and sounded for many days in an effort to recover his body. But neither the body nor the bottom of the lake was ever found. Since that time a metal barricade has been erected to prevent others from falling."

"But the barricade could be removed?"

"Yes, it is possible."

"Then—"

But Neric was on his feet. "Raamo," he said, "I can see the wisdom of what you are suggesting, and I fully agree with you. I can think of no better answer—no better final resting place for this thing, which has already caused so much evil. But it does seem to me that we would be foolish to be too hasty. It seems to me that we would be foolish to destroy the weapon while Axon Befal and his followers are still unaccounted for and still equipped with tools-of-violence of their own making. Do you agree with me, fellow Councilors?"

Around the table-board, most of the Councilors seemed uncertain, their eyes moving nervously from

Raamo to Neric and back to the thing that lay gleaming in its nest of withered grundleaves. At last someone spoke.

"I agree with Neric," an Erdling Councilor said. "Now that this great power has fallen into our hands, why should we give it up until we have found Axon and removed the threat under which we have been living?"

"Until we have removed the threat?" Raamo asked. "Do you mean that you would use the tool-of-violence?"

"No, no, of course not," the man said. "I would not use it. But it seems to me that its existence might be enough to prevent the Nekom from using their sharpened staves and levers."

"The Councilor speaks wisely, Raamo," Neric said. "And don't forget, Axon may still be holding the children prisoner, even though the time has passed for their ransom. If the children are still alive, it seems to me that Axon would be much less inclined to harm them if he knew we had the tool-of-violence."

Eyes turned to look with sympathy at Kanna and Herd and then back at Raamo and again to Neric. Neric was standing tensely erect, his eyes gleaming with the strength of his conviction, while Raamo only stared at Neric dazedly, as if confused or bewildered.

"Speak, Raamo. Make them understand," D'ol Falla was thinking when the boy turned suddenly and looked directly into her eyes, and she found that she was pensing his answering thought.

"It is no use," he told her silently. "It has won. They will not deny its right to be. And it will always win until it is denied."

Torn between a wild rush of Joy that the Spirit-gift had returned to her after so many years, and the bitter despair of Raamo's message, D'ol Falla sat as if stunned, immersed in inner turmoil; but all around her the Councilors were beginning to nod and gesture towards Neric to signal their approval.

Kir Oblan was the first to be recognized. "I find myself agreeing with Neric," he said. "It will be time enough to rid ourselves of the tool-of-violence when——"

But Kir's speech was interrupted by a sound so strange that all other thought was wiped from the minds of those who heard it. As one, they turned in its direction.

The sound, halfway between a scream and a strangled sob, had come from Genaa, who was still supporting the sagging figure of the serving woman. Genaa was standing now, her face bleached and contorted. Gently lifting Maala from her chair, she turned her around so that her back was towards the council-table. In the center of the serving woman's back, something darkly wet was oozing through the silk of her shuba.

"What is it?" Maala said anxiously. "What evil has it done to me? Tell me what it is?" She had begun to unfasten the shoulder ties of her shuba, but her fingers were trembling so violently that Genaa had to come to her assistance. When the stained silk was, at last, lifted away, no one spoke, but the air throbbed with silent echoes of shock and horror.

D'ol Falla rose from her chair, and going to Maala spoke words of comfort and hope. "Peace, peace, Maala. Try not to tremble so. We will take you to the chambers of healing, and all will be well with you. Wounds heal, Maala. Surely this wound, too, can be healed."

A litter was sent for, and Maala D'ach was carried from the assembly hall. For some time after she had gone, the Councilors sat in stunned silence. But when at

189

last the speaking began again, it was directed towards one matter only—the best and safest way to transport the tool-of-violence to its final resting place in the bottomless cavern.

The planning moved forward with great efficiency, hastened perhaps by the Councilors' obvious desire to remove themselves from the vicinity of the ancient weapon. A few agreed to guard it through the night, by standing watch outside the doorways of the hall; and others left for Erda to bring back a heavy metal urn in which the weapon and its contaminating power could be contained. On the following morning, it would be carried to the cavern of the Bottomless Lake.

CHAPTER NINETEEN

Raamo came to D'ol Falla's chamber very early the next morning, soon after the last fall of rain. He came to speak to her before he left to take part in the procession that would accompany the tool-of-violence to the Bottomless Lake. The journey would be long and arduous, and only those Councilors who were strong and vigorous were expected to go. D'ol Falla would, of course, remain in the Vine Palace, but Raamo wanted to see her before he left.

"You are pensing again," he said as he held out his palms in greeting; and her eyes glowed with Joy.

"Yes," she said. "In the last few days there have been hints—wisps and shadows—but yesterday in the hall there was no doubt. It was strong and clear."

"Yes," he said, "I know."

"After so many, many years. And for it to happen now, in the midst of such great trouble. I can't understand it."

Raamo smiled. "It might have happened sooner if it had not been for the thing that was hidden in the cage of the joysingers and in your thoughts. It would have happened sooner if there had been no need for hiding."

191

"Yes," she said. "I thought of that, also. I think you are right." The boy's gaze met hers, and she pensed his shared delight at this gift that had been returned to her after so many years. For an amount of time that seemed fleeting and yet endless, she was once again caught up, lost, and freed, in the intensity of mind-touch.

Later, when Raamo was preparing to leave, he spoke of the woman, Maala D'ach. "Do you think it is in the power of the healers to help her?" he asked.

"Poor woman," D'ol Falla said. "I spoke to her of healing, but I am not certain. I have never seen such a wound."

"Kir Oblan said it resembled the wounding caused by fire," Raamo said. "But how is it that she was wounded simply by carrying it on her back? Others have handled it without harm. And your joysingers lived above it for many months."

"I don't know," D'ol Falla said. "But Hiro thinks it is possible that its materials have begun to decompose with age. And perhaps the jarring motion of constant carrying hastened the disintegration so that the force with which it is empowered began to leak out. There were forces used on the ancestral planet that had such corrupting powers."

"Yes," Raamo said. "I think Hiro is right. It leaks an evil, now, that corrupts the body. But it has always leaked a more deadly evil."

"Yes, but that will soon be over, Raamo. Before this day is done, it will be gone, and forever."

"I don't know," Raamo said. "The Council agreed to do away with it because they were afraid. But they did not deny its right to be. I am afraid . . ." He paused, and D'ol Falla saw that his eyes were unfocused and inward, as if turned towards far-distant sources. After a time he went on, "Without their denial, its power will not be destroyed."

"I am afraid . . ." he said again, and turned away; but at the doorway he turned back, smiling, and sang the parting.

The procession to the Bottomless Lake was the strangest that Orbora had ever seen. The ancient weapon, now tightly sealed in a heavy metal urn, was strapped to a litter with greatly extended carrying poles. The litter was carried by teams of bearers, who were changed every few minutes. The Councilors who had agreed to accompany the procession were divided into two groups, one to proceed and one to follow the litter and its deadly burden. A procession, by long tradition, symbolized glory and honor, and was conducted in an atmosphere of triumphant Joy. But this procession was grim and silent; and fear, like an unseen canopy, hung heavy about it.

There was, of course, reason enough to be afraid; but the deep, pervading apprehension that surrounded the procession was beyond reasoning. If anyone had questioned them, some of the marchers might have said that they feared the mysterious contamination that had wounded the serving woman and that might not be wholly contained inside the metal urn. Others might have said that they feared the procession might be in danger from an outside source. If Nekom informers had been at work during the hours of darkness, there was the possibility of an attack by the followers of Axon Befal.

Hiro D'anhk, leading the procession with Ruula D'arsh and Kir Oblan, told himself that he feared an explosion. From what he had learned of the ancient sources of power, it seemed possible that a long fall and the shock of striking water—or a projecting rock— might cause a cataclysmic release of power that could entomb them all.

Walking with the group of Councilors who followed the litter, Neric's mind surged with the fear that they had made a mistake in deciding to rid themselves of the weapon so hastily. There had been no attempt to discover if its leak of power could be controlled—and if it would still function if the Nekom did, indeed, attack the city.

But Raamo felt fear as an evil ghost of the past. The fear that had made their ancestors refuse to give up the power that had, at last, consumed them. It seemed to Raamo that the fear spreading out around the metal urn was almost willed into being by the thing inside—by something alive and sentient and determined not to relinquish its ancient authority.

The journey was not quickly accomplished. It began on the Lower West Branchway of Hallgrund and made its way to the new stairway that, circling Halltrunk, led down to the forest floor. From there the party went by winding surface pathways, where dense growth pressed close on either side, and fern frond arched, lush and green, above. Skirting the surface city of Upper Erda, they came at last to the mouth of a tunnel, and a loading platform for railcars, which now ran all the way from Upper Erda to the caverns of the old underground city. A train of seven cars was waiting, and when the urn had been placed in the central car, the Councilors boarded the others. It was while he was waiting for a chance to board that Raamo became aware of the fixed gaze of a young man with a wide flat face and wild, unruly hair.

The young man was not the only person who had been following the procession. Processions were traditionally followed, and this one was no exception, although these followers were grim and silent, rather than joyful. They did not press close in their efforts to see, but only continued to follow, at a distance, and with a strange, patient persistence. At the loading platform they came somewhat closer, and it was then Raamo realized that he had seen the flat-faced youth before.

When the train was finally loaded, the young man was still on the platform, but some time later, when the rail journey was over and the procession continued, once more on foot, the followers appeared again. And once more, the flat-faced boy was among them.

The journey went on and on. The tunnels narrowed, and the glowing wall torches became fewer and farther between. At last they stopped altogether and there were only hand-held lanterns to light the way. The tunnels turned and twisted, narrowing at times to mere crevices, and then giving way to enormous caverns where water dripped endlessly down slimy walls and grotesque formations hung down from above like organic growths.

Chilled by the deep, dank cold and burdened by exhaustion and ever-growing fear, the Councilors at last saw before them a grillwork of close-set metal bars. Near the grill a crew of Erdling metal workers waited. Their flaming torches revealed a narrow gap in the barricade, where several bars had been removed. Behind the grill the flickering torchlight struggled against a wall of darkness, revealing, now and then, a black nothingness, sharp-edged and sudden, beyond the wet gray rock of the cavern floor.

The bearers slowly approached the barricade, and

195

placing the litter in front of the opening, they stepped back quickly into the crowd of Councilors. The Councilors stepped back also, back and back, until they had retreated halfway across the cavern floor. The urn sat alone, and the torchlight reflected by its burnished surface made it seem to glow with a pulsing inner light.

Raamo looked around him. All the Councilors, men and women, Kindar and Erdling, were staring with fear-glazed eyes at the urn and the darkness that lay beyond it. He could feel their terror growing and spreading like a living thing. And he knew that although they called their fear many names and gave it many faces, in the end it was the same fear that had caused their ancestors to shape the evil the urn contained—and then refuse to deny it until it was too late. If something were not done, and quickly, it might be too late once more; they would find reasons to retrieve the urn from the edge of oblivion and carry it back with them to Green-sky.

Suddenly he was walking forward, past Neric and then past Kir Oblan and Hiro. The straps that held the urn fell away easily, and he lifted it in his hands and stepped through the opening in the barricade. Behind him there was a rush of sound as the Councilors surged forward, as far as the barricade. The light from the torches leaped wildly and then stilled, and all sound died away. He moved forward slowly over wet and slippery rock.

The rock sloped steeply downward to where, only a few feet away, it ended in the sharp-edged slash of darkness. Tiny streams of water trickled past his feet and slid silently over the edge to disappear forever into the lake that waited far below.

Raamo walked slowly and with great care. He reached

the edge, and when he was certain that his feet were firmly planted, he leaned forward and extended his arms, to hold the urn out over the darkness of the crevice.

But the thing in the urn was not yet conquered. Its power still lived and took strength from the minds and Spirits behind him that had not yet denied it. A numbing indecision gripped him, making the urn seem to cling to his hands. He struggled to release it; and in the struggle, he slipped forward and plunged over the precipice.

He was frightened as he fell, but the urn was still in his hands, and as the waters of the lake closed over his head, he saw with a clear fortelling that the evil in the urn would be denied in his memory, and his name would become a talisman against it for many years to come.

To those who were present—the Councilors, the Erdling workmen, and those who had followed the procession—the time that followed was a wild confusion of hopeless effort and strangely violent sorrow. There were screams and moans, people who ran uselessly in circles demanding that something be done, and others who sank quietly into motionless mounds of grief.

Ropes were finally produced; and Neric, screaming and shouting orders, insisted that he be lowered down over the rim of the precipice. And it was done. The rope was not long enough to bring him near the dark surface of the lake, but by the light of the lantern that he carried, he was able to see the water below him was as smooth and untroubled as if it had been undisturbed for a million years. When Neric was drawn back up over the rim, he had ceased to shout, and he was not the same.

There came a time when they knew that there was

nothing more to be done, and all sound and motion stopped except for quiet weeping. The people stood quietly, close together, touching each other for comfort, and stared through the iron grillwork towards the dark slash of the crevice. They had stood thus, quietly, for some time, when suddenly someone cried out, as if in pain, and a figure pushed forward.

Hiro was standing near the opening in the barricade. As the one who had cried out pushed past him, he saw that it was a young man, and that his wide flat face was violently contorted. The young man stepped through the opening before Hiro could reach out to stop him. For a moment he seemed to be fumbling with a large carrying pouch at his waist, and then he took something from the pouch and held it high above his head. Perhaps a foot long, metallic, and sharply pointed, the thing gleamed in the torch light. Then the young man threw it fiercely towards the chasm. It struck the rocks at the rim with a loud clanging sound and then plunged over into the darkness. When it was gone, the youth crumpled to the floor and began to sob and moan with wild abandon.

They pulled him back, then, behind the barricade, and Hiro tried to question him; but he was hysterical and almost incoherent. They were able to learn only that his name was Dergg and that he had something to tell the Council. So they took him with them on the long sad journey back to Orbora.

That night, weighted down by exhaustion and sorrow, the Council heard the story of Dergg Ursh—and with it the story of Axon Befal. Dergg Ursh, they soon saw, was a simple, graceless boy, who was not at ease with the more complicated forms of spoken language. But it was impossible to doubt that he spoke sincerely. And the message that he brought was of utmost importance.

"I was always lonely," he told the Council. "I was lonely in Erda, and in Upper Erda. My parents died when I was very small, and I had no true clan, so when I was asked to join the Nekom, I felt that at last I had something to belong to. Something important and strong, so that someday people would look up to me and give me honor.

"At first when I joined the Nekom, I was only a secret member. I was told to go on working at the lapan-house where I had been so that I might feed and shelter the members when there was need of it. And so I did.

"But one night, at the lapan-house, Axon Befal spoke of something that frightened me and almost made me wish I was not a Nekom. He spoke of how he had tried to attack Raamo . . ."

Dergg's voice broke, and for a while he struggled to regain his composure. When he went on, there were tears on his cheeks and his voice trembled. "But Raamo got away; and I was glad, because I saw him once, and when I saw him, I knew that he was good. But later that night Axon Befal sent me away because he was going to speak to some of the Nekom about a great new plan. And when he had told them, there was an argument with much shouting, because some of the Nekom did not like the plan. I heard Axon Befal shout that if they would not help him, he would do the plan alone.

"Then I did not see Axon Befal for some days; and when I saw him again, he came to the lapan-house all alone. He spoke to me with great kindness and listened to me talk, and then he asked me to come with him to the forest and be a real Nekom, not just a secret one.

200

So I went with Axon Befal into the forest.

"But when we got to Axon Befal's city, I was surprised because it was not a large city, and many of the nid-places seemed to be empty. It was after that that Axon Befal told me what had happened—how his great plan had been to steal the holy children and take them away into the forest so that the Council would be forced to listen to him and do what he said. But some of the Nekom did not like the plan. That was why there had been shouting, and Axon Befal had said that he would do it alone.

"But he did not do it. Axon told me many times that he did not do it. Because when he was almost ready, he heard that someone else had already stolen the children.

"But on that very day—the day that the children were taken—Axon had gone out alone into the forest to look for a place to hide the children. So all that day no one had seen him, and when the Nekom heard that the children were gone, some of them would not believe that it had not been Axon who took them. So some of them were angry, and they went away from Axon's city and took most of the wands-of-Befal away with them. And the city was almost empty.

"On that night, the night that I came to the city, Axon talked to me for many many hours. We drank many tankards of pan-mead together. And he told me over and over again about his great plans, and about how evil and treacherous it had been of the Nekom to go away and take his wands-of-Befal. I was honored that the Great Leader would speak so long to me alone and share his thoughts with me. And I swore to him, before the morning came, that I would not desert him and that I would follow his orders no matter what he might ask.

201

"So by the next day Axon Befal had made a new plan; he would send a message to the people of Orbora saying that he had taken the holy children, even though he had not. Because they were gone and the people of Orbora would not know that he had not taken them. Before they found out that he had not, he would be in the temple, and all the power and glory would be his, and mine also, because I had been brave and loyal. So I carried the message for him to the newsinger, and we waited to hear that the Council had sworn to serve him and had obeyed his orders.

"But nothing happened except that the rest of the Nekom went away from the forest city, and we were left alone. Then searchers began to come into the forest, and we had to leave the city. So I went back to work in the lapan-house, and I hid Axon Befal in the back of the pantry behind some bales of lapan fur. He stayed behind the bales during the day, but at night when the light was dim, he disguised his face with a false beard and came out into the hall of food-taking to talk with the people who had come to eat lapan.

"Last night Axon Befal heard that the Joined Council was going all the way to Erda and the cavern of the Bottomless Lake. And he made a new plan. His plan was that I should follow the procession, and that I should—"

Once more the boy was overcome by sobs. Tears ran down his cheeks, and his blunt, unformed features twisted into a grotesque mask of grief, but he did not turn away or hide his face.

When he was able to go on he said, "His plan was that I should creep up behind Raamo—and that I should strike him with a sharpened tool—so that he would die.

Axon Befal said that if I did it carefully so I was not seen, the Kindar Councilors would blame the Erdlings, and the Council would destroy itself. Then there would be much fear and confusion, so that people would turn to Axon Befal as a great strong leader who would help them and take away their fear.

"I did not want to do it, and I asked if it could be some other besides Raamo. But Axon said no, because no one else was important enough, and besides, if Raamo lived, he would turn the people against us. So he made me swear a great oath. He said it was an ancient oath of great power, and if I broke it, I would die. I swore the oath, and I went out to wait for the procession.

"When I saw him, I could not strike him. But I was afraid not to because of the oath. So I followed, not knowing what I would do, or not do. Then in the cavern when I saw what happened, I knew. I knew that Axon Befal had told me to do an evil, evil thing, and I knew that I was evil for thinking that I would do it."

The boy had begun to sob again, and his voice came in choked painful gasps. "If I die of the oath, I will be glad. I only wish that I had thrown myself into the chasm—with Raamo—instead of only the evil tool."

CHAPTER TWENTY

The enormous amphitheater was full to overflowing. The rising ranks of benches were packed with people, and in the semi-circle before the central stage, a dense sea of humanity covered the forest floor.

It was the day that was to have seen the Celebration of the Rejoyning. A full year had passed since the holy children had taken the tool-of-violence from D'ol Regle by means of the power of uniforce, and the Geets-kel had renounced D'ol Regle and embraced the cause of the Rejoyners. But there was to be no celebration.

The people had come together to mourn the loss of the holy children. And to mourn also for Raamo, who only six days before had taken the tool-of-violence into the dark waters of the Bottomless Lake.

For six days the people of Green-sky had been in mourning. The Erdlings, long familiar with suffering and loss, had learned a new and purer grief, and the Kindar had found tears, which had been denied them for generations. For six days they had shared the age-old torments of loss—the tragedy of what might have been, the torture of if only, and the sad mystery of why. And on the

204

morning of the day that was to have held the Celebration, they came quietly to the amphitheater to share in a ceremony of mourning.

Above the crowd, high on the central stage, D'ol Falla waited and watched the gathering of the great multitude. She had been asked to speak to the people, and her speaking would be the beginning of the ceremony. But she did not know what she would say. There was no Kindar ritual for grief or sorrow, and she did not know the Erdling ceremonies.

There were many sad things that could be spoken of. She could speak of Hearba and Valdo, the parents of Raamo and of Pomma, who were now childless and ill of grieving. She could speak of her own sorrow and of her fear that all hope had been lost with Raamo. But when the time came for the ceremony to begin, and Hiro led her forward to the front of the great platform, she still had not decided what it was that she would say.

At the platform's edge she stopped and looked out over the great multitude and up at the small hanging stages where newsingers waited to relay her words so that they would reach the farthest fringes of the crowd. And words came into her mind as if through a far distant pensing.

"Let us rejoice," she said.

She saw and felt the shocked astonishment, beginning all around her and spreading outward as the newsingers repeated her words again and again like receding echoes.

"There has been much to mourn for," she went on, "and we have mourned. I, too, have sorrowed—and blindly—so it was only now, only this moment, that I saw what lies before our eyes. Look! Look around you. You have come together, a vast multitude, without fear

205

and suspicion, and you have comforted each other with touching and with the sharing of tears. Truly, we are rejoyned, and we have done it alone—with only the power that lies among us."

She paused, and the people looked at each other, some in bewilderment and some in dawning recognition.

D'ol Falla would have spoken further, but at that moment the crowd's attention was distracted by a gliding figure who, swooping down steeply from far above, was circling directly over the amphitheater, as if looking for an opening in which to land. Heads were shaken and there were mutterings of disapproval. It was inexcusable that a late-comer should choose to arrive at such a ceremony in so distracting a manner.

Then the gliding figure banked sharply and dropped suddenly to a landing on the hanging platform of a newsinger, sending the platform into such wild gyrations that the newsinger was almost pitched off into the crowd below. Indignant gasps and even angry shouts came from all over the amphitheater. But then it became obvious that the newcomer, a Kindar woman, was speaking to the newsinger in a highly agitated manner. It was suddenly apparent that the intruder's rude arrival was due not to thoughtlessness, but to the urgency of the message she had come to bring.

Finally, the newsinger turned and lifting his hands high above his head in a gesture of rejoicing, he shouted, "The children are found. The holy children are safe and well. The children have returned."

The other newsingers took up the cry and spread it to the farthest edges of the crowd, and for several minutes there was a great joyous confusion. All over the amphitheater there were shouts and cries, tears and laughter, and on the great stage all the members of the Joined Council crowded around Teera's parents, Kanna and Herd, to share in their happiness.

When the confusion had, at last, died away, it was seen that the woman messenger had been summoned to the stage and was being questioned by the Chief Mediator.

And then, in turn, Hiro spoke to the multitude and told them what he had learned.

"This woman is Ciela D'ote," he said. "Serving woman to the D'ok family in the Vine Palace. She stayed today in the palace to care for the parents of Raamo and Pomma, who were still too ill from grief to attend the ceremony. Around the tenth hour, after all the others who dwelt in the palace had departed, a group of children appeared at the gates, and with them were the lost ones, Pomma D'ok and Teera Eld. And so Ciela was sent here to tell us that Valdo and Hearba are coming to the amphitheater by way of branchpath and stairway and will bring the children with them.

Amid cheers and cries of Joy, Kanna and Herd came down from the high stage and set out to meet their daughter. But the Chief Mediator asked that all others remain in their places; and so they waited quietly except for a high-pitched hum of whispered anticipation. Many questions remained to be answered, but when Hiro questioned Ciela further, he found that she knew little more than she had already revealed.

At last there was a stirring far to the rear of the crowd, heads began turning, and then a group of figures appeared at the far end of the center aisle: four larger figures and around them a dozen smaller ones. As they came nearer, the people could see that it was true—

the holy children of the Rejoyning had been returned to them. Before the eager eyes of the multitude, they walked down the long aisle: the fragilely beautiful Kindar child, and the dark and vivid daughter of Erdlings, living symbols of the Rejoyning and of the people's faith in Spirit-power.

They mounted the great stage, and the parents of the holy children led them forward, not only Pomma and Teera, but the others also, to the edge of the high platform, where they might be seen by all the people. They stood close together, their faces solemn, and some of the younger ones hung their heads in fright. Several of the children were clearly of Erdling parentage. They ranged in age from a girl of eleven or twelve, to two little boys who were no more than four years of age. There were no shouts or cheers now; but all over the amphitheater, the people rose, both Erdling and Kindar, and extended their arms in the gesture of welcome.

For only a minute the children stood before the multitude, and then they were led through an entry arch to the waiting and robing rooms behind the great stage. When they were gone, Herd Eld spoke briefly to the Joined Council and then came forward with Hiro D'anhk to the place of speakers.

"It has been decided that Herd Eld will speak to us of what he has learned of the disappearance of the children and how they came to be restored to us."

So it was the father of Teera who told the story just as he had heard it from the children—of how in the days following the Rejoyning, Teera and Pomma's lives were greatly changed, and when they had a little time in which to play their old games, they found they had forgotten much that they had taught each other. They had been

saddened to find that they were no longer able to pense or image; but when they realized that they might never again be able to summon the power of uniforce, they began to be tormented by fear and guilt.

Without a true understanding of why it was so, they knew that the adulation of the people, and also in some mysterious way, the future of the Rejoyning depended on their ability to merge their Spirit-force in such a way that things of apparent solid and heavy natures would be moved and changed. They believed that sooner or later they would have to go before the people and demonstrate that ability—and they knew, now, that they would fail. So they began to feel deceitful and guilty, and after a time, the Vine Palace, which had seemed so great and glorious when they had first been taken there to live, began to seem more and more like a prison where they awaited the inevitable disclosure of their guilty secret. And then one day they heard that the time would soon come when they would be asked to go before the people, and it was soon afterwards that they asked Teera's clan-sibling, Charn, to help them run away.

For the past month, and all during the time that the far reaches of the forest had been searched for them daily, they had been no farther away than the Garden, the old Orbora Garden, which Charn had once attended. Charn had taken them there because of a hidden place, which he had helped to build, between the grundbranches that supported the garden floor. It had been a good hiding place, quickly accessible to the children of the secret troupe that had been formed to care for the fugitives—to bring them food and also to provide them with almost constant company and entertainment. This troupe, made up of Charn's special friends and some younger siblings who were admitted because they had discovered the secret, made life very pleasant and exciting for the two little girls who had been, for such a long time, without the company of other children.

There had been times when Pomma and Teera had remembered their parents with guilt and grief; but they had begun to experience faint signs of returning Spiritforce, and so they had waited, hoping to recover the power of uniforce.

But then, only five days before, the children had come to them with the terrible news of Raamo's death; and for a time Pomma had been ill with grief. So they had waited until she was able to speak and reason, and then, only that morning, they had started for the palace. But the secret, roundabout route that Charn had planned, took longer than they had expected, and they arrived too late at the palace, after everyone had departed for the amphitheater, except for Ciela and the grieving parents of Pomma.

When Herd finished his story, and the farthest newsinger had repeated the last phrase, an uneasy silence descended. The people looked at each other uncertainly. The children had been restored to them, but they had come back no longer the same. They had gone away living symbols of hope, and had returned—as children.

Then D'ol Falla came forward again to the place of speaking, and the people turned to hear what she would say.

"I had begun to speak to you of the power that comes from among us," she said, "and of seeing that which has long been before our eyes. I have seen only now what I should have known long ago—why it was that Raamo spoke so often against the adoration of the children. We

211

have heard how a great burden was placed on them by forcing them into the role of symbols. But I see now that we harmed not only the children, but ourselves as well. I see now that Raamo's warning was for the danger of letting our hopes rest on the powers of great leaders, of outside forces, however strong or holy, when, instead, our hope should have been in the power and strength that comes from within and among us, and from our birthright as Kindar.

"For we are all born as Kindar and ever have been. We are all born innocent of fear and hatred, and innocent, also, of limitations and barriers. We are all, at birth, greatly Spirit-gifted, perhaps in ways as yet unguessed. And the Rejoyning will come, in the end, not through Rejoyners, nor Councils, nor even through miracles, but through accepting the powers and responsibilities that are our birthright. And when that time comes, we will all be, simply, the Zhaan, the people—the one people of Green-sky."

When D'ol Falla ceased speaking, the people were quiet. She pensed that their minds were full of hope, but also of a weary understanding of the long path that still lay ahead. And D'ol Falla, herself, felt suddenly very weary.

Hiro D'anhk had come forward to speak to the people. He spoke solemnly of things accomplished and of things yet to be done. But D'ol Falla found that she could not listen. She had done her part, and she was too old and tired to do more. So she left the great stage, moving quietly so she would not be missed, and went back among the robing rooms to look for a place to rest and be alone. But she found instead the room in which the children were waiting.

212

The room, which had been designed to hold materials necessary for ceremonial functions, was quite large and lined with shelves and wardrobes. In the open space in the center, the children were seated close together on the floor, except for the two littlest boys who were playing near the farthest wall.

D'ol Falla had entered quietly, and for a moment no one seemed to be aware of her presence. The oldest of the children, a Kindar girl of perhaps twelve years, was speaking in a low earnest voice. She broke off, suddenly, and rising, she crossed the room to lift the little boys down from the shelves on which they had been climbing. It was while she was returning to the circle that she noticed D'ol Falla.

"Look," she whispered, "the old one."

The children turned, and immediately Pomma and Teera ran to her and embraced her, and Charn followed only a few steps behind.

"Did you come to get us?" Teera asked apprehensively. "Do they want us, now, out there?"

"No," D'ol Falla said. "I was not sent for you. They are busy speaking and will be for some time to come. I was only very tired and looking for a place to rest."

A low stool was found and placed near the circle of children, and when she was seated, they crowded around her, except for the little boys, who had gone back to climbing. The others looked up at her with anxious faces, and she pensed their concern for many things that they did not fully understand.

She began to speak to them comfortingly, assuring them that what they had done would be understood, and that they had not caused evil or harmed the Rejoyning. They listened earnestly and with great attentiveness, ex-

213

cept that Charn left the group briefly to once more lift the little boys down from a high shelf. The Kindar boy, a flower-faced infant with thick bright curls, sat down docilely upon the floor, but the Erdling boy clung to the shelf in protest until Charn pulled him free.

"Stay down from there, Brant," he said, "before you harm something."

"That one is Charn's brother," Teera told D'ol Falla.

"And the other one is my brother," the oldest girl said. "They want to see that urn on the highest shelf. I told them to stay down, but they've never seen a thing like that before."

D'ol Falla went on speaking of how it was possible that the disappearance of Pomma and Teera had been, in some ways, helpful, since it had shocked the people into a silence that had permitted listening. And from the listening had come the beginnings of understanding. She was not sure that they understood, but she knew that they were comforted, and she felt that she, herself, was comforted and her weariness somehow lightened.

And suddenly that lightness began to grow until it became a great flowing force. D'ol Falla felt herself turning with it to face the far wall of the room where the two little boys were sitting side by side, their faces still and intent and their arms stretched out before them. Above them, the great marble urn was drifting slowly through the air.

The older children watched until the urn had reached the floor, and then they turned away as if they had seen nothing strange at all. Breathless with sudden Joy, D'ol Falla sat motionless, until Teera leaned forward, her face glowing with the delight of a shared secret.

"Shh," Teera whispered. "We haven't told them yet. They still think it's only a game."

214